THE WHITE TRAIL

FFLUR DAFYDD

THE WHITE TRAIL

NEW STORIES FROM THE

MABINOGION

SEREN

for Iwan and Beca

Seren is the book imprint of
Poetry Wales Press Ltd
57 Nolton Street, Bridgend, Wales, CF31 3AE
www.seren-books.com

© Fflur Dafydd 2011

ISBN 978-1-85411-551-5

A CIP record for this title is available from the British Library.

Cover design by Mathew Bevan

Inner design and typesetting by books@lloydrobson.com

Printed by Bell and Bain, Glasgow

The publisher acknowledges the financial support of the
Welsh Books Council.

Contents

New Stories from the Mabinogion

Introduction

Some stories, it seems, just keep on going. Whatever you do to them, the words are still whispered abroad, a whistle in the reeds, a bird's song in your ear.

Every culture has its myths; many share ingredients with each other. Stir the pot, retell the tale and you draw out something new, a new flavour, a new meaning maybe. There's no one right version. Perhaps it's because myths were a way of describing our place in the world, of putting people and their search for meaning in a bigger picture that they linger in our imagination.

The eleven stories of the *Mabinogion* ('story of youth') are diverse native Welsh tales taken from two medieval manuscripts. But their roots go back hundreds of years, through written fragments and the unwritten, storytelling tradition. They were first collected under this title, and translated into English, in the nineteenth century.

The *Mabinogion* brings us Celtic mythology, Arthurian romance, and a history of the Island of Britain seen through the eyes of medieval Wales – but tells tales that stretch way beyond the boundaries of contemporary Wales, just as the 'Welsh' part of this island once did: Welsh was once spoken as far north as Edinburgh. In one tale, the gigantic Bendigeidfran wears the crown of London, and his severed head is buried there, facing France, to protect the land from invaders.

There is enchantment and shape-shifting, conflict, peacemaking, love, betrayal. A wife conjured out of flowers is punished for unfaithfulness by being turned into an owl, Arthur and his knights chase a magical wild boar and its piglets from Ireland across south Wales to Cornwall, a prince changes places with the king of the underworld for a year…

Many of these myths are familiar in Wales, and some have filtered through into the wider British tradition, but others are little known beyond the Welsh border. In this series of New Stories from the Mabinogion the old tales are at the heart of the new, to be enjoyed wherever they are read.

Each author has chosen a story to reinvent and retell for their own reasons and in their own way: creating fresh, contemporary tales that speak to us as much of the world we know now as of times long gone.

Penny Thomas, series editor

The White Trail

Cilydd

It was on a day when Goleuddydd was at her most visible – more visible than she'd ever been in her life – that she seemed to vanish into thin air. How could you lose a pregnant wife in a supermarket? That's what people were asking. Cilydd watched the news item every night in a stupor, as if he were watching a story about someone else, as if it were some other unfortunate being he saw snivelling into his fleece at the press conference, eyes at half mast. 'We are all concerned for my wife's safety,' he heard the sap say. 'She is nine-months pregnant and very vulnerable.' Very vulnerable. How Goleuddydd would have hated that. She had never been vulnerable in her life, let alone invisible. She wasn't a woman you could miss, a splay of wild red hair twirling like a tornado around her small, perfectly formed face, a woman who walked in bold, quick strokes; it was always you who had to step aside, never her. But, as she had prophesied, the pregnancy changed her. As she grew bigger and bigger she somehow retreated into herself, became half the woman she had been, even as her flesh doubled. Her red hair stood static on her head, became a matted pink mess. She walked as though trudging through treacle, the whole world around her a gloopy, arduous struggle. She was all too visible and yet ever so slowly disappearing.

Something wasn't connecting, she told her husband. Neurons were misfiring all over the place. She had dreamt awful things of late; had seen her baby shrunk to the size of a die, imprinted with dots. One night, Cilydd woke to find her shining a torch on the wallpaper, and when he asked her what she was doing she told him she was looking for the join of flesh and concrete – for she had dreamt that the baby had been built into the foundations of their home, squished in between two bricks. The most persistent, recurring dream was the one where she left the baby on a pub windowsill and, when she returned, found that the taxidermist had been at it, mounting her offspring on the wall: a dream which left her uneasy for days.

In the final month she began taking down all the pictures in the house, in case they fell on her pregnant belly. She wouldn't take a bath because she was afraid the floor would give way beneath her. It seemed that everything she had previously known and trusted; every static, fixed, screwed-on thing was now malleable, rickety, unreliable, including herself. And Cilydd, too, seemed to fit into that category.

'Is it me you want or just the baby?' she would ask him, sloping off before he could answer. Whenever he tried to reach out to touch her stomach she would stare at his hand as though it were a hostile creature, swatting it quickly away. 'Is it kicking? What does it feel like?' he often asked her. 'Hard to describe,' she'd say, before giving him a sly pinch in the ribs. 'Something like that, I suppose, only firmer. Harder.'

A stylist by trade, it seemed that she could find

nothing that would soften or style her bump, favouring rather the unflattering smocks that were her mother's hand-me-downs, merely emphasising how laborious and irritating the whole ordeal was to her. 'Why are they all staring at me?' she'd say. 'Why do they all seem to think they can speak to me? Baby this, baby that. Do you know what you're having? Why does it matter to them what I'm having? What I'm having, everyone, is a nervous breakdown.'

Which wasn't a mile away from the truth, Cilydd began to think. It was in the genes, she said; hereditary. There had been that incident with her grandmother and the maypole. Her mother and the suspension bridge. But so far none of them had made a run for it. He knew that's what the police officers were thinking when he reported her missing. 'She's left him, hasn't she? Made it look like a disappearance. Poor bugger.' And the longer she stayed missing, the more certain he, too, became, that whatever had happened to his wife, she had brought it upon herself.

It had been a Saturday afternoon. She was wad-
dling around the cheese aisle at the time, perusing
all those pearly triangles she'd been denied for so
long, staring at the blue threads of Stilton as though
they were her own veins. He was at the checkout
(buying snacks for the maternity ward, sugary lolli-
pops to help her in labour, little treats to help him
through the night, and those maternity essentials for
the things no one wanted to think about) and, as
there was still no sign of her by the time he reached
the entrance, he waited by the toilets. After thirty
minutes he'd grabbed the elbow of a tiny, white-
haired pensioner and pleaded with her to go in and
check for him, and when that proved unfruitful he'd
gone back to the car. He'd sat inside with his snacks
and breast pads reading the fine print on the pack of
maternity towels, before scouring the supermarket
one last time. There was an announcement going off
repeatedly, calling someone to the flour aisle, and he
wondered for a second if he should request such an
announcement for Goleuddydd. But he could imagine being scolded for it later on. 'So embarrassing,

Cilydd, to have my name called out like that as if I were some missing toddler.' And so he left it, went to his car, and drove home.

Leaving the supermarket, he felt an overwhelming sense of relief, as though he were leaving the whole sorry situation behind. She's at home, he thought with great certainty. He was convinced of it. Of course she's at home. But when he arrived home the house was dark and empty. He sat there until all the light had drained from the room. Goleuddydd. Her name a combination of light and day; those bright, hopeful things. He recalled how last Christmas, in the days before the pregnancy, she had beckoned him to the window to see the sun rising over the snow, her face alight with childlike wonder. She was always showing him the light in things, the whiteness. When they first met it would pain him when she left the room, as though the light were leaving too. The day she disappeared happened to be the shortest day of the year.

Of course the whole thing became a spectacle. It was Christmas. The silly season, with no hard-hitting news to speak of. Which is why a pregnant wife's disappearance became TV gold. Much was made of her love of cheeses, the brokendown CCTV camera which cut out at the crucial moment, and of the argument he and she may or may not have had in the car park, which was really just a hair tousle (him), and an attempt to snatch a snowflake (her). These gestures, exacerbated by the fact that, according to one of his neighbours, they hadn't been getting on, of course made the whole thing appear rather suspicious. Much was also made of the thin air into which she had vanished. As it happened, this was not thin at all; but thick and glutinous, dressed in tiny white particles. In the wake of his wife's disappearance, the flour aisle curiously burst its banks, spreading tiny atoms of spelt, buckwheat, tapioca and rye into the stale air of the supermarket. No one seemed to have witnessed it happening. The few shoppers in that particular aisle only remembered the sudden sensation of flour-on-the-lungs, the uncontrollable cough, before tiny pale hillocks appeared mysteriously at their feet. Nobody actually recalled seeing the flour fall. When the bags were examined it was found they had all been punctured sharply and swiftly, though it was impossible to tell by what. Some other items were missing, too, some bread had gone astray, and some of the shelves also seemed pockmarked. Cynddylig and Tathal, the flour-aisle security guards, were actually on a sandwich break when it happened.

'The holes and the indentations,' the detective told Cilydd, 'may prove to be a significant feature of our investigation.'

This, of course, did not provide any consolation for Cilydd. He wanted something real and concrete to go on, to tell the rest of the family, to hold on to in those dark, lonely hours. A small hole was not enough. At his request, he was shown the CCTV footage again and again, watching his wife turning that fateful corner. The cheese-aisle security guard – Gorau – was reprimanded for his lax surveillance. 'I'm paid to watch the cheese, not the people,' he protested.

They replayed the incident in the flour aisle too,

looking for clues. The atomic eruption seemed to happen spontaneously, leaving grainy trails over the camera surface.

'Could there be a fault with the tape?' he asked. The policeman pressed rewind. Cilydd watched the white fug retreating back into the little brown bags. Chaos retreating into calm. On another screen – at the very same moment – Goleuddydd reappeared.

'There would appear to be some sort of time-lapse here,' said the policeman. 'The supermarket tells us there isn't. That it's linear, continuous footage. But we think they're hiding something. I mean, there might have been a robbery, and for some reason – we can't think why just yet – they're trying to cover it up. So perhaps your wife, in some way, was caught up in it all.'

There was nothing for Cilydd to do but wait. His father-in-law, Anlawdd, was on the phone daily, shouting at him to get things moving. A formidable figure, a former chief constable, he had never thought Cilydd – a lowly loss adjustor – good enough for his stylist daughter. 'It's an adequate first marriage,'

Cilydd overheard him saying to one of the guests on their wedding day, 'but let's hope there are no offspring and that we can move on from this nasty business with minimal damage.' From the second Goleuddydd told him she was pregnant, it seemed Anlawdd was waiting to catch him out, to bring the whole thing to an abrupt end, and to claim his daughter back as his own. Cilydd could see him working away at her during her pregnancy, a cup of coffee here, a lift there, until she was staying overnight at her father's house on a weekly basis. 'He's taken such an interest in this baby,' she would say, while Cilydd knew full well that the interest was not so much in the baby but in controlling the *damage*, as he would have it. And now the damage was colossal. It had started with the undoing of his daughter's fine, shapely body, and had now ended in her obliteration in a supermarket on a wintry afternoon, while everyone else was staring at flour dust.

'She's got to be somewhere!' he shouted at Cilydd down the phone. 'Don't snivel at me, Cilydd, just do something about it. Get that cousin of yours on to it. Lord knows he needs something to crack on with. I always knew this marriage would come to no good.' Cilydd heard the reluctant gunge of grief in his father-in-law's windpipes. 'I'm just very, very worried that something awful has happened here. So get that cousin of yours to look into it. Right now. I shouldn't say this really, having been in the force myself, but don't bother with the police.'

The cousin Anlawdd referred to was Arthur, Cilydd's private-eye relative whose business was anything but private. He lived on the main street of the town, with only his first name printed on a plaque outside his house. ARTHUR, it said, in bold, gilded letters, against a red-painted backdrop.

'It's ambiguous, don't you think?' Arthur always said, flicking his dishevelled fringe over his left eye. 'I mean, just giving one name like that, without any details underneath. They see it and they don't think – accountant, lawyer, physiotherapist. They know I'm something else. But they won't bother to find out what until they really need me. So it's a win-win situation. Completely conspicuous but somehow entirely ambiguous at the same time.'

Whenever you asked anyone on that busy main street what the 'Arthur' referred to they told you it was the house of the local private eye, and that he'd not managed to solve a single investigation since he'd started practising. They would also tell you he'd tried his hand at a million other things too, all of which had been unsuccessful. Carver, painter – candlestick maker. The only thing he'd been any good at, they would stipulate, was working as a street artist a few decades ago. His sketches were said to be uncanny likenesses, whipped out of the stub of his pencil in minutes.

It was evident even from the state of Arthur's house – his *HQ* as he called it – that his methods left something to be desired. Here was a man who'd been searching for a whole host of missing persons for twenty years and who couldn't find so much as a clean knife in the kitchen. He ushered Cilydd in, between huge stacks of dishes, books and shirts that seemed to be looming in every corner, waiting to topple. The walls were covered with newspaper clippings and pictures of missing persons – they stared out at Cilydd from every corner of the room – hundreds of pairs of lost eyes which Arthur, as far as he knew, had never been able to locate. Accompanying most of these were Arthur's own sketches of the missing – some of them a myriad of images of the same person ageing, over time; the guessed faces becoming dense with age, crinkling in charcoal. It sent a shudder down his spine to think of his wife, and maybe even his baby ageing, minute by minute, even as he was ascending the stairs now.

And yet there was a kind of feverish excitement about Arthur which made someone believe that if enthusiasm were the only thing needed to solve a crime, he could do it. He had created a space in the living room, forging a little clearing in the mad woodland of his life, where he'd placed a pot of coffee, two surprisingly clean, new-looking cups, a notebook and some pens. Cilydd sat down and was surprised by how the day fell in through the skylight, illuminating, it seemed, only this particular corner. It was a light untainted by the dirty greying sky above – light that made him think of Goleuddydd. Suddenly, staring at the crisp paper, the concave china mouths waiting to be filled, seeing Arthur's pen poised with sincerity and hope – it seemed possible that Goleuddydd and his child could be brought back to him.

'I mean, there are bound to be other private eyes working on this, but they won't have the inside info that I have – they won't be hearing it all from the horse's mouth,' Arthur said proudly, passing the sugar bowl to his cousin as though he were expecting him to take one of the sugar lumps in his mouth and neigh his appreciation. This was the moment at which Cilydd realised Arthur saw Goleuddydd's disappearance as rather a piece of luck, something that gave him an edge over other private eyes in the area.

Cilydd learned that his wife's case seemed to match another disappearance in a town fifty miles to the west. If they could crack this one, Arthur said, his eyes gleaming with hope, then it was likely to be the key to a major operation happening somewhere. Which could certainly guarantee that his reputation would be somewhat restored.

'A fourteen-year-old girl disappeared just like that – from her bedroom. She was up there, listening to music, but when they called her down for supper, she was gone. When they examined her room they found these peculiar little dents in everything and her magazines had been torn to shreds.'

'So what are you saying?'

'I'm saying they might be linked.'

'And what about the money?' he asked.

The police had told him that Goleuddydd had taken a rather large sum of money out of her bank account the day before her disappearance. He caught the policeman and policewoman looking at each other as they told him this; it was as though a gust of cold air had blown into the room. The information changed their attitude towards him; the police-woman's hand on his went limp. He found them sweeping him with their eyes – trying to work out exactly what it was about him that was so over-whelmingly *present*, to make a woman want to be absent.

'No, there was no money missing in this case. But the girl had been acting strangely for a few weeks, according to her family. Look, just let me look into it. Trust me.'

Cilydd trusted nobody. As the days wore on, the likelihood of Goleuddydd coming back to him diminished. The light and day of her name drained from him in thick, ugly sobs. He stopped answering the phone to Anlawdd, who left angry messages which overran the tape of the machine. He sat in the dark most evenings watching the traffic going by, watching cars slipping and sliding on the black ice, wondering where in the cold world Goleuddydd and his baby were. So she had done it; she had escaped from him, like she had joked she would. And it seemed unfair that there was no escape for him. She was everywhere. In all the papers. The photos he gave the police were all of a pre-pregnancy Goleuddydd. Her beauty and boldness took your breath away. 'Fears mount for missing beauty', one headline roared. He could not bear the thought of her beauty becoming ink stains on jam-sticky breakfast thumbs, of Goleuddydd entering every single household but her own.

Every now and then he went for a walk in a nearby seaside town, walking out across the cliffs to a small island which was always deserted. You could cross over when the tide was low, but you had to be quick, otherwise you might get caught there. He stayed a little longer every time. Until the dark waters started to seep over the bridge of land – which he saw as the bridge back to his life – before deciding to return at the last minute. He knew the tide of his grief was rising, and that it was only a matter of time before he would stay put on that island. But he wasn't ready yet. He couldn't do it while there was still hope Goleuddydd would overcome whatever madness had taken hold of her and come back to him. And in the absence of a body there was still a chance that his baby's ferocious beating heart – a lovely heartbeat, the midwife had said at their last appointment – was still echoing some-where in the world.

And when they finally came – three police offi-cers, two men with furrowed brows and a woman whose face was a fixed, constant apology – to tell him they'd found his wife's body, the first feeling he experienced was one of vindication, of righteous-ness. Rather than give in to true, genuine grief, which twisted his innards with biting ferocity, he found himself engaged in a rather elaborate tirade at the police, before fainting into the lap of the female police officer at the end of the garden path, clutching on to her curtains of blonde hair. They brought him inside and gave him hot, sweet tea. It was the classic antidote to trauma – he'd read all about it in his birth book – a short, sharp elixir of caffeine and sucrose. Even as he was drinking it he wondered how an elated father would approach the steaming cup. He wanted to pour it all over himself, let his emotional pain be replaced with a physical one. Instead he politely gulped it down and burnt the roof of his mouth.

'So you've found her,' he said.

'Well, yes, we've found her. And I'm afraid she's...'

'Well she's dead, obviously,' he muttered, imagining the foetus hibernating inside, never to be roused from its lair. 'I always knew she was going to be dead.'

'Yes, she's dead, and I'm very sorry for your loss. But I'm afraid it's more complicated than that...'

More complicated than death? What could be more complicated than the sudden termination of a life that had been thirty-three years in the making? He thought suddenly of paperwork, his wife's clothes, books. What do to with them all? The traces of a life suspended, as though the person would return at any moment. These thoughts were followed by more unpleasant ones – he thought of that abundance of red hair, her lovely smooth shoulders, the scar on her little finger; what would become of those?

Then he looked up into the officer's dolorous eyes and suddenly understood what they meant by *more complicated*.

'Oh, I see. I know. She was pregnant. So it means,

two funerals, I suppose. Does it?' He wasn't sure. Or would it merely mean a bigger casket? Again, he was trying his best to appear sensible, to take control. 'Two caskets?' he said, looking up, in a tone that could very well have intimated something quite ordinary, like: 'two biscuits?' By striving for ordinariness he had reached the register of hysteria now, a semi-tone away from suspicion. The police officer told him to slow down, to take his time.

'It's about the baby,' the male police officer said before looking meaningfully at the female police officer. 'There are some things we need to discuss about the baby she was expecting.'

'My boy,' Cilydd said. Goleuddydd had told him, after the second scan, that it was a boy. Had he imagined her smiling then, knowing he had wanted a girl? He suddenly regretted not accompanying her to the hospital, to see his boy's first tumble through the dark. But then, she hadn't wanted him there. He had felt entirely separate from the pregnancy all the way through, as though it were nothing to do with him. The female police officer moved closer to him, until she was practically on his lap. He inhaled her sharp, floral perfume; wrinkling his nose in distaste. Why did they always push a woman on the bereaved? The doe-eyed creature stared at him and grappled with his hand.

'Yes, the boy. He wasn't, he wasn't there when we....'

The police woman's hand crept up his sleeve.

'Will I have to register him? Formally I mean?' he asked, pushing the hand away.

'Sir, I'm afraid there was no baby. She'd been, she'd been... there is no easy way to say this, sir. She'd been cut open. I'm afraid your wife may have been the victim of foetal theft.'

The words made no sense to him. Foetal theft. A foetus in a bag. Men in balaclavas looting around in someone's abdomen?

'Someone's taken the baby. It looks as though the whole thing was premeditated. Whoever did it may have had some experience, but we have to be realistic here – in the absence of medical attention we don't hold out much hope for the baby having survived. But the thing is now, to find out who did this and...'

'But my son... my son *might* be alive?' Cilydd asked.

'It's possible sir, yes, but...'

His son might be alive. It was the only thing that truly registered. Suddenly to be still missing seemed a glorious thing.

'But why?' he felt his throat constricting now with the anticipation of grief. 'Why would someone do a thing like that?'

'Well, we can't say for sure, but these days there are all sorts of people just desperate for a baby. I suppose they just, well, they must have seen their chance.'

The female police officer tried slinking an arm over his shoulder; he got up just as she was doing it, so that she fell slightly into the sofa. He went to look out of the window, at the garden gate that he had seen Goleuddydd coming through hundreds of times in his life. These past nine months he had seen her struggle with the latch, sometimes heaving herself over it, just to make things difficult – knowing he was watching. Wanting him to know what a sacrifice it was being pregnant, with its million inconveniences, with this slowly ballooning body. He couldn't quite believe that he'd never see her walk up that garden path again.

'We'll let ourselves out,' whispered the female police officer. 'We'll be in touch.'

Cilydd insisted on seeing where they'd found the body; the police stressed that there was no need for him to go. But the *need* they talked of was something they would never fathom; an abhorrent, insidious force in the dark folds of him, which drove him to want to experience every last shred of her undoing. He wanted to fill his lungs with the last air she had breathed, to feel the ground that had given way beneath her feet.

Arthur rang to ask if he could accompany him; Arthur, who was now full steam ahead with his investigation, the details of which he couldn't disclose. 'I'm starting to put it together,' he said feverishly, excitedly over the phone, 'I feel that I'm on the verge of great... of a great discovery. Just play along with the police – they never solve anything; they simply go through the motions. But I'm getting closer, Cilydd. I will get you back your boy, I promise you. Don't tell them I'm a private eye, will you?'

He remembered nothing about the journey, only how short it was – it seemed that the grey streets gave way to green pastures in seconds, and all too soon they were approaching the scene, the sun shining too brightly for such a dark day. He was vaguely aware of a conversation going on between Arthur and the policemen. Goleuddydd was not mentioned by name. She was merely 'the victim' – even Arthur, he ascertained, was talking of her in such terms. They talked of the vulgarities of a body he didn't recognise – a slit there, a gash here – that was not Goleuddydd. Goleuddydd was a living, breathing, complete being. At what point would she have become the victim? The second she left the supermarket? Or would it have come later? Perhaps it wasn't until they cut into her flesh that she truly knew. He recalled how wilful and spirited she had been at times in her pregnancy. Had it even been forced upon her? Or was it some sort of game? 'My dreary husband's in there buying my maternity essentials; take me away from it all will you?' He could hear her saying it – asking to be abducted. Getting into a car with a complete stranger. Sticking her head out of the window as they sped out of the car park, sticking out her tongue to lap up those dirty snowflakes. Arthur and the policeman were still babbling on – *victim, vulnerable, time of death, botched Caesarian*; the new, awful vocabulary of his life.

They drove up a dirt track, rounding the corner into a farmyard. The farmhouse was grey and decaying; pale green moss creeping up the walls like bad facial hair, a monster of a building. There were some disused tractors and farm machinery lying about, metallic skeletons gawping at him. It was a place drained of colour – cold and chalky, at odds with everything Goleuddydd stood for. He tried to imagine what she had felt when she'd taken all this in. Maybe that's when it hit her; that to be in the supermarket on a Saturday with a husband who loved you wasn't such a bad thing, compared to this. The policemen began walking towards a small, dark heap at the far end of the yard. It wasn't until it was right in front of him that he saw the cluster of stones for what it was – a circular pigsty. No one spoke for what felt like a long time. It was only when Arthur gave him a nudge that he realised what they were all waiting for – for him to go in, on his hands and knees, to shuffle down on his trotters, like a pig. The police officers bowed their heads, before handing him a torch.

He was surprised by how big and cavernous it was inside. Positively luxurious, he imagined, for swine. Not so for a nine-month-pregnant woman.

'Is this it?' he hollered. He sensed the aroma of something else there amid the dust and dirt, something too awful to think about.

'Yes, sir. That's where we found her.'

Inside it was just a dark, stench-ridden hole. He wondered where she'd been lying; remembering the size of her, her physical awkwardness those last few months. It must have been a tight squeeze. Did she know she'd never be coming out?

'Why here?' he hollered again to the police officer. 'Why leave her here?'

'We don't know sir,' the police officer muttered. 'This is what we're trying to establish.'

'I can smell pigs,' he said.

'Some of the samples of saliva on your wife's body do show that she was... she was... in the company of pigs at the time of death. But we can't find any traces of the animals I'm afraid. And this farm has been abandoned for quite some time.'

'What do you mean "in the company of pigs"?' Arthur asked. Cilydd could hear the frantic nib of his fountain pen, gushing blue veins all over his white pad.

'Pig saliva was found on the body,' one policeman stated. 'But like I said, we're not sure where the pigs came from.'

Arthur inhaled sharply: an inhalation of pure excitement.

'A link,' he said, knowingly.

'A link with what?' said the policeman.

'Never you mind...' Arthur replied.

'Sir, with all due respect, if you have any information you should...'

'Oh no... just an observation... Cilydd, are you OK in there?'

'Yes,' Cilydd said in a low voice he no longer recognised as his own. His eyes were still getting accustomed to the darkness. He was lying on his back now, as he presumed Goleuddydd would have been when it happened. In the earlier, healthy days of her pregnancy, she had told him that she wanted to be upright for the birth. 'How nature intended,' she said. It wasn't much to ask for – the simple pull of gravity.

'Cilydd, can I come in?' Arthur asked.

'Not yet,' he said.

He opened his eyes. The dark was clearing now, and it was surprising how darkness took on a new, transparent sheen once you got used to it. Even the smells were commonplace. *In the company of pigs*. It seemed so absurd, so very unlike his graceful Goleuddydd. He switched on his torch and let the tiny ball of light roll across the grimy roof. And then, suddenly, there it was, etched on to the stones.

'Don't remarry,' it said. Written in blood. He let out a sharp gasp.

'He's seen it,' he heard someone outside saying. 'Sir, is everything OK?'

Don't remarry. It was his final contact with Goleuddydd. He reached his hand towards the ceiling, towards her. His hand was left cold and empty – the dried blood did not leave a mark on his skin.

'The blood...' he started.

'Yes, I'm afraid the blood on the ceiling matches your wife's blood, we've checked this,' said a voice from outside. Cilydd lay back, turned off his torch. He lay there for some time. Two police officers came in and took both his arms trying to squeeze him back out through the entrance. It was only then he realised how long he'd been in there, for it had gone dark outside. There was no light to be seen, bar the fluorescent stripes of the policemen's uniform, and the occasional glint of Arthur's teeth. Dark inside and out, he thought: this is all that's left of me, a hollow pigsty of a man, who will emerge from one kind of darkness only to fall into another, and then another, and it would be ongoing blackness from now on.

★

And so there it was; a dead wife, a missing – presumed dead – baby, and nothing left to him in the world but a scrawled message on a wall, a Palaeolithic punch-in-the-guts which was undoubtedly written by his wife's hand, the looping D, the slanting, unserious Y. It was just like her – to lay claim to her personality even as life dripped out of her; only she could make that last drop of blood count. Cilydd turned it over and over in his mind – was that really her last thought – he mustn't remarry? He thought of all the messages she could have written on that wall. She had never been a jealous woman, but then again, he had never given her any reason to be. There was nothing for him but her, nothing at all; if she was the light, then other women were mere shadows. Why should she care if he remarried? But then, who was to say what anyone would write when the last of their blood was draining away? If one could choose just one final word, one final utterance, how was it possible to choose something truly profound, something that would really communicate? But then he saw the cleverness of it. She had gone for something which could not be misunderstood. No one would ask, but what did she mean, what did she *really* mean? What she meant was, *don't remarry Cilydd. I strictly forbid it.* He could hear her voice saying it, wryly, her lips scrunching up.

And there it was: his wife's full stop on his life, which rolled at his feet like some omnipresent cannonball. He could not go back; and he could not go forward. The media, which had been so interested, moved on. The police had to accept that they were stumped. The farm where his wife's body was found was sold to a young family. The supermarket offered him a year's supply of home deliveries – which he accepted, merely to avoid having to face that aisle ever again. There was always Arthur of course – ringing him up every now and then – sitting him down in the white space in the flat, making him go through the details of other disappearances, presenting him with more and more sketches, scribbling his son into existence with a charcoal pencil every now and then. But soon it felt as though what had happened was no more than a story and, like most stories, it had come to a rather dissatisfying end.

And so Cilydd once more started going for long walks to that tiny island, following the lure of the land further and further out towards a foaming, frothing fate. But still he raced back, against the tide, at the very last moment. It had been a year or so, not long enough, he told himself, to completely give up hope.

Something was needed to fill the hours while he waited. He could not do something as menial as go back to work (the fact that he was a loss adjuster resonated painfully now that he realised no amount of adjustment ever really covered a loss), and so he decided to take what they were offering him – *compassionate leave*. How crisp and clean it sounded, tinged with the promise of restoration, like a good night's sleep in a hotel bed.

But he had no time for compassion. Or for leave. There was only one thing for it. His missing son, slowly but surely, became his calling, and he found himself part of a new world – the world populated by those left behind.

It was only a quick computer search that was needed to confirm that half the world, it seemed, was missing. Cilydd started to attend groups, listening to people regaling their own tales of loss. Soon he was volunteering to become the treasurer of the Missing Persons' Network. Then a secretary. Before he knew it he was spending every night typing up the profiles of missing persons on to the website. And it helped him – being able to lose himself in the details of disappearances which were just as awful, just as baffling, in some cases, as his son's. The work did not upset him. He dealt with it clinically, matter-of-factly, as though he were back in work. In many ways, he had merely become another kind of loss adjuster.

After three months at the helm, the website was more substantial than it had been in some time. Those at the Missing Persons' Network said they could not imagine a time without Cilydd. He was needed. Recognised. Commended even. He scanned back through his work almost nightly, memorising all of the profiles, particularly the names of any sons that had gone missing. There was the case of Greidiol Gallddofydd (last seen walking dog on the promenade, wearing only flip-flops), Graid son of Eri (last seen leaving a fairground with a hot dog in his hand), Cubert son of Daere (last seen getting into a taxi wearing his wife's bathrobe), Ffercos son of Poch (last seen going to the toilet at a restaurant), Gwyn son of Esni (last seen doing up his shoelaces outside a newsagent's) Gwyn son of Nwyfre (last seen at the barbers, laughing and joking), the two brothers Gwyn and Edern, sons of Nudd (last seen having a picnic on a beach) and Cadwy son of Geraint (last seen buying stamps), not to mention Fflewddwr Fflam Wledig, Rhuawn Bebyr son of Dorath, Bradwen son of Moren Mynog, and Dalldaf son of Cimin Cof, who all left nightclubs tired and alone, dancing their drunken way into the abyss.

He spent hours scanning in their photos – face after face stared back at him from holiday snaps, amorous embraces, party clinches, work dos – tens of smiles which revealed no trace of that urge to walk into the blackness and leave everything behind. And these images made it even more difficult for him to complete his son's details – who, in the absence of a photograph, had to have the ubiquitous head and shoulder box attached to his equally anonymous, nameless profile, accompanied by a question mark, plastered over the face like some horrendous birth mark.

He listened to fathers lamenting the loss of their sons; men he could imagine had once been robust and fearless, but who were now ground down to ghostly impressions of themselves, their jackets loose about them, trousers frayed at the edges, facial hair trying to mask the disappointment that was etched into their faces. But the more he listened, the more alone he felt. Every single story had its roots in a known presence, there was someone who had lived, who had been, who had filled a space, and who suddenly was no more. He was the only one who missed someone he had never met. Whom he could not even be sure actually existed. And worse still – who had no name. At the beginning of every meeting the members of the group stood up and said their children's names. They learnt quickly enough to let his turn pass. Still he felt it – that nameless presence, surfacing like bile in the back of his mouth, and there was nothing for it but to swallow the emptiness back down.

Years passed. Arthur would ring him every time a child went missing, asking if he saw any similarities. Yes, he would say. A child's gone missing and some-one's world has been gutted from the inside; there's your similarity. Cilydd kept his eye on the news for stories of missing children. He envied some parents their resolutions, even if in some cases it ended with a badly mutilated body at the bottom of a ravine. A corpse was at least something, he thought, thinking of Goleuddydd lying on her slab in the morgue. But something much darker lurked in him when he heard of children being found safe and well, even against the odds. He was jealous, and he wanted the child to go away again. He wanted the child to be dead.

Every Christmas he organised the Missing Persons' Network minibus down to the Assembly, where they all went to hang the name of their loved ones on the Christmas tree. Some Assembly Members came down and talked to them in serious voices, then disappeared back up the stairs to get on with their business. A minister shook hands with them, as though congratulating them all for some huge feat.

One morning Cilydd woke to the startling realisation that he himself had become a missing person. That all this talk of absences had rubbed off on him, and that he had somehow become absent from his own life. It seemed that no one looked at him in the street anymore, no one called his name. Sometimes, the air that surrounded him seemed so joyless, so thin and insubstantial, that he forgot to breathe, until his lungs lurched forward and forced him to. The more he thought about it – the more he realised his life was over now. It had run its course. And that's when he decided that he was finally going to do it – remove himself from life, and make his absence official – a permanent state. Before the day was out. As the hours ticked on, he felt incredibly restless. He'd heard of the serenity that befell suicidal people when they were about to kill themselves, and yet he possessed none of it, he was a fidgety, bumbling mess. He dropped his keys into his cereal; he could not decide which shirt to wear, he tripped over some loose carpeting and hit his head on the corner of the coffee table, nearly taking himself out before he'd even left the house. To try to calm himself, he started on some paperwork for the Missing Persons' Network, filling in some of the most recent profiles – he could not bear to leave things undone, and it focused him for a few hours, at least. Then he felt the necessity to write a few letters, just in case his body was never found (for he could not bear to be missing out of spite, to leave others in the lurch) – writing one for Arthur, one for Anlawdd, and another general note to the members of the Missing Persons' Network, informing them of his intentions, telling them not to give up hope, though he realised how fruitless and depressing the whole act would be; what impact it would have on them. He then ambled his way to the cliff tops just before dusk, posting all three letters on his way (with a second-class stamp, so as not to arrive too early), and before he knew it, he was there, on his island. He looked behind him and realised that the tide was too low to claim him yet. He had come too early. Then again, what was the point in waiting? For all he knew the tide could well decide to deliver him back to shore. No, if he was going to do this, he had to do it properly. He clambered up onto a rock near the cliff face and stared down into the water.

He stood there, poised at an angle, wondering how he would do it. Birds circled around him – dark birds which came in clusters, egging him on. He shooed them away and stared down once more. What if the shock of the water was not enough? Should he try to make sure he hit a rock on the way down? What if he only hit his head or his leg – and ended up drowning slowly in still waters, in horrific physical pain? No matter how much emotional pain he had endured over the past few years, the notion of actual bodily pain, the externalisation of all the grief and loss he had endured still seemed unbearable. He thought again, reluctantly, of Goleuddydd's womb being torn open, and those pilfering, reddening fingers taking his son. That was when he decided he would have to make his own end as tortuous and painful as hers.

Then – just as he was about to do it – a shadow crept across the rock. He was aware of someone breathing behind him, someone – he guessed – who was too afraid to make his presence entirely known in case he were to startle him. Cilydd was inches away from a fall. Don't look back, Cilydd told himself. Once you get engaged in a conversation, that's it. He moved closer to the ledge. But the silhouette moved along with him, inch by black inch.

Cilydd held his breath. The waves beneath him were ferocious swirls, sickening him. Just as he lost his balance, he heard a rustle of fabric, and a flash of something familiar caught his eye. Something urged him to see the person behind him before he fell, in case they had something to tell him. Perhaps it was Arthur or Anlawdd, breathless with news after all these years – *they've found him*, the words that echoed around his head daily, the faint echo of hope that was always there.

But perched on that rock was not Anlawdd or Arthur or anyone who even remotely knew him. It was someone who looked familiar but whom he could not place – a rambler who, in seeing Cilydd's head turn and his shoulder sway slightly towards him had made the brave decision to try to reach out and save him. And all Cilydd did was slap his hand away, one light, fly-swatting move which was enough to make this robust rambler lose his balance, and before either of them knew it, it was the rambler who was tumbling down over the rocks, banging his head on the rocks below (Cilydd closed his eyes and heard the awful coupling of rock and bone) before his body thundered into the water. Cilydd lay down and listened to his heart thumping through the rock. Behind him a wax jacket lay limply in the place the rambler had once stood. Something beeped in the pocket; vibrations of life pulsing through the fabric. Cilydd got up and ran – running over the tiny bridge of land, just as the tide was coming in – running in wet shoes all the way back to his car, his mind racing, his veins full of adrenalin. He felt alive. Terribly, awfully alive, and present; he put his hands to his chest, felt the rhythm of his heart, felt his pulse, all the necessary things that kept him from disappearing and suddenly he was glad that it had not been him. But how to undo what he had done? This man had interfered, he thought. This man had brought it on himself. But the more he saw the man's face leaning forward towards him, that palm outstretched, the more he was convinced that there was something familiar about him.

He couldn't contact the police. One phone call and he would be culpable, though in actual fact he'd done nothing. Nothing but be foolish enough to believe he could actually kill himself. He started the car, and drove out of the car park. All the while his mind swished and swayed with the dark waves, those very dark waves that were, at every moment that now passed, carrying the rambler's body further into the grey void of the sea.

He did nothing. He went back to his house and sat all night at his kitchen table. Someone would find him now, Cilydd thought. The ubiquitous man and his dog, whose early morning walks would never be the same.

And before the end of the week was out (a week spent undoing his so-called suicide, collecting his suicide notes from the postman before they could reach their destination, hiding in Anlawdd's bushes, stalking the pavement outside Arthur's flat) he knew who the man was. It was Doged, the health minister, whom he had met once at the Assembly. He read the story in the papers, saw his widow – a rather good-looking woman – staring back accusingly at him from the front page. He remembered Doged as one of the ministers who'd been particularly kind to them, who had sat and listened to several of their stories with real feeling, or so it seemed, while the other civil servants around him looked on, bored and expressionless. So there it was – he'd managed to top the health minister, of all people, bringing the uncommonly healthy Doged to his sudden death through his own ill health. All the papers claimed he was missing, of course. They still hadn't found a body. But the abandoned wax jacket and Blackberry seemed to confirm things. 'Health minister missing; feared dead.' There was also a cluster of white shells found on the precipice (for all Cilydd knew, he could have kicked them there himself), which might be significant, one journalist claimed, before going on to suggest that Doged had probably left a suicide note spelt out delicately by shells, but that the wind had rearranged them, making it impossible to pick out his message. Even more intriguing was his wife's insistence that he had meant to kill himself. 'He had not been happy for some time,' she was quoted as saying. 'The pressures of a top job. The ill feeling towards him in the constituency over the closure of the local hospital.' Cilydd had seen none of that in that outstretched hand, the rosy, well-meaning face. The more he thought of it, the more he realised that Doged had actually looked him in the face as he fell, that there was a winged grace to him, a glint of Icarus in his eye.

But it was his wife's second comment that made him sit up and take notice. 'He always said that if anything happened to him, I was to remarry. Of course it's too soon to think about such a thing now, but it just goes to show the generous spirit of the man.' *Do remarry.* Perhaps that was what Doged had spelt out in tiny patterns of shell, before the wind scattered his good intentions. Cilydd saw it as some sort of sign.

The next day, he urged the secretary of the Missing Persons' Network to contact Doged's widow. Before the week was out, he was shaking her hand. Gwelw she was called – a name that suggested no more than a ghostly outline of a woman. Yet somehow she exuded warmth, right to the tip of her cold fingers. Doged had been good to them, he told her, they would like to help her, and her young daughter

(Lleuwen, her name was, suitably, a moon-surface of a girl, pearly and blotchy in turn) to get through the next few months. Gwelw started attending their meetings. She stood up and said Doged's name, peacefully, as though she had already let him go. When he told his own story, ('My name is Cilydd, my pregnant wife was abducted and murdered and her abductors took my baby') her hand found its way into his: a soft, comforting creature, which he tried to lure into his grasp again and again.

Her own grief seemed short-lived; her husband, after all, had killed himself, she told the group. He had chosen to go. How could she even lament the loss of one who wanted so desperately to be dead? If she truly loved him — she told them — then she should be happy. Happy for him that he had come to his desired end, and that she would be moving on with her life. Once her eyes rested on Cilydd when she said this. He was jolted by it; and for one moment it felt as though she looked right into him, and saw the film that was permanently playing in his mind, of Doged tumbling through the air. She knows, he thought irrationally, she knows. But she didn't, of course. The look, the one she fixed him with week after week was actually tinged with desire, and in a bizarre twist of fate he found himself, after one particularly morose meeting, making love to her in a secluded spot in the community-hall car park. It was the most wildly irresponsible and impetuous thing he had done since he had inadvertently pushed her husband off a cliff. When he came it felt as though the whole world thundered beneath his feet, the ledge disappeared, and the world clicked back into place.

Curiously, after that, he did not think much of his part in her husband's death. He began falling in love with her. She was the complete opposite of the volatile Goleuddydd, a woman who thought about things, who did not wear her beauty boldly, but who hid it behind a dark, slick curtain of hair – who smiled only when she thought something well and truly funny, a kind of smile you had to fish for in her unquantifiable depths, and which, when it surfaced, seemed like a reward, a pearl in the hand. She was an orthopaedic surgeon; effortlessly brilliant, and saw things with precision and clarity; as though she had an innate x-ray vision. She spoke in careful, measured language, not in expletives and hyperbole as Goleuddydd had – when she was positive she was 'encouraged', whenever she was keen to do something she told Cilydd that it was 'probably appropriate'. She was clinical and beautiful, some-how the woman he'd been looking for all his life. They understood one another – for she, like him, had lost someone. And he wanted to marry her.

Although his wife's command was still fresh in his memory, still as starkly unmistakable as ever – over the years it had accumulated invisible clauses. He convinced himself that what Goleuddydd had meant to say was: don't remarry unless... Unless you really fall in love. (Which he had – helplessly, passionately.) Unless there is some deep desire in you to have another baby. (It was at the front of his mind, though he wondered whether Gwelw, at 42, was rather beyond such things.) Unless that is the only thing that will save you. (Doubtless that – unless he found someone to ward off the emptiness with him – he would end up back on that ledge.) And another one of those unlesses would surely have stipulated that it was OK to marry a widow, one who had been through the exact same miserable grief as himself, even if he had unwittingly eradicated her husband so that he could find a way to survive. *Unless it's absolutely essential Cilydd*, Goleuddydd would have said, *then don't*.

But if you must, the bunches of her red hair would have rustled.

And so at the end of the year, with Doged's body still drifting in the sea somewhere, Goleuddydd's fiery light was replaced with the more demure rays of Gwelw and Lleuwen. The wedding was a modest affair. A register-office ceremony with a few witnesses and then a reception at a boutique hotel with a few close family and friends. Arthur was the only one Cilydd could think to invite. He turned up with an enormous gift lapped in lavish gold wrapping paper, beneath which was a striking canvas portrait of Cilydd, Gwelw and Lleuwen that he himself had painted. Cilydd looked up at his cousin in gratitude and read the relief in Arthur's eyes. The portrait was a means of painting over the past – and Arthur had done so with a flourish.

Though the bond between himself and Gwelw's nine-year-old daughter was rather strained at first, Cilydd was determined to forge a relationship, if only to fill in that last gap in his life. She needs time, Gwelw said. She had adored Doged. She had been his little shadow. They needed to make sure she felt loved and wanted and that she understood families changed, they were renewable things; that that's how life was. Sometimes mummies and daddies, for no good reason, died or disappeared and when that happened then someone new came in their place.

'Don't patronise me,' said the nine-year-old girl. 'I know why you and my mother got married. It's so you can feel better about yourselves, and better about what happened to you.'

'Well, that's true, but what's also true is that I love your mother very much...'

'I read about you on the internet. How someone

killed your wife and took your baby. It can't have been nice.'

'It wasn't nice, no,' Cilydd said, wincing. 'But it was a long time ago. Before you were born. And when something happens before you were born, it doesn't really affect you, does it? So if you think of how little it's affected you, then that is how little it affects me, now, really. I've forgotten all about it. I'm starting a new life, a new family, with you and your mum.'

'Taking advantage of the fact that my dad's dead, you mean.'

'Not at all,' he said, wishing there had been less mention of Doged in the wedding speeches. The memory had begun to resurface. Now it was back in his consciousness, and he had to do his very best to keep it at bay. Whenever he thought of him, he'd immediately think of something banal like bananas or sausages, and he'd force the words to come cantering across his brain in various flashing colours, knocking Doged over at every opportunity. His mind was becoming more and more like some educational kids' TV show, as though he were learning how to think, how to remember and forget, all over again. Doged, someone said. Bananas, Cilydd thought.

What kind of stuff did she and her dad do together, he asked her. She looked blankly at him. She said sometimes her father would take her to the Assembly and some of his staff would take her for a walk around the Bay. Once she went on a carousel, a memory that seemed lodged in her mind as one of the most wonderful things they had done together, despite the fact that it was a young intern who was holding her coat at the side and waving at her, while her father was deliberating on the privatisation of hospitals. The more he found out about Doged, the more he thought he was right to do what he'd done. I will not feel guilty about it, he thought. No one will ever know. And then the final consoling thought, which kept him going when nights were dark and the demons of guilt and condemnation wandered up from the depths of his subconscious – *one day everyone who ever knew Doged will be dead and none of it will matter. Everyone is going to die. Doged, Goleuddydd, his son, they were going to die anyway.*

And this is how Cilydd trundled on, in his makeshift, imperfect existence, believing that the life he was now living was the one he was meant to live. Gwelw and himself tried for more children, but nothing came of it, and in the end it didn't seem to matter. He had helped raise Lleuwen, after all, and that was enough for him. Once she went off to college, he and Gwelw spent their free time going to galleries, drinking elaborate coffees like caramel mochaccinos and soya frappes, having friends round for dinner, and generally being happy. Yes, one day, dare he say it, Cilydd found himself thinking that he had created the best he could out of an unfortunate situation and made a life for himself. People never now referred to him as 'that guy' – the one who had lost everything – as they did in the early days of his courtship with Gwelw. Now he was merely Gwelw's husband, Lleuwen's father. Life was being lived and he had managed to squeeze Goleuddydd, his son and Doged's unfortunate end into a tiny portal in his brain, whose door only ever opened when he was asleep, and even then, it would only creak its way ajar, and just a small smattering of that startling light would be visible.

Gwelw and himself still dallied in the business of missing persons, attending meetings, giving the odd speech here and there, but it became an increasing burden on them to be intimate with the relatives of missing persons, who reminded them too much of their former, grieving selves. They would rather not think of people in their lives who were still missing (though neither of them truly thought of Doged as a missing person – more as a floating carcass at large in the world), and they almost found it embarrassing to be involved with the network; to be dragged down by it. Gradually, their involvement stopped. Cilydd erased all the files from his computer and passed the baton on to some other poor soul – a man whose wife had gone missing from a routine trip to the dentist's. And he went back to being a loss adjuster – filing claims, and finding the ordinariness, the greyness of his anonymity much easier to bear.

And that was when the phone calls started. A voice, which seemed familiar, in the thick of night which asked if Cilydd was at home and if he was ever going to tell his wife what he'd done to her beloved Doged.

And then a click.

The phone calls would only ever come when he was home alone, as though the caller were careful not to alert his wife or his step-daughter, as though he were being watched closely. The line was unclear – a faint crackling could be heard, obscuring the voice. He began dreading being on his own, to the point where he would insist on accompanying his wife wherever she went, much to her annoyance. Her evenings in with friends would often be darkened by his presence, lurking, in the car or in the hallway, insisting he was fine with his book, to the amusement of her friends, who could not believe a husband could be so possessive. When his daughter came home from college he would drive her to meet her friends in town, and pretend to go back home for the evening whereas in reality he was sitting in his car, in the cold, thinking about a phone ringing in an empty room. And his daughter would nearly always spot him, come out of the pub and ask him what he was doing. He would see her friends at a table in the window; immaculate, confident girls with honeyed hair, hiding their smiles in their pale yellow wines – laughing at him. Both his wife and his daughter tolerated the situation with tight, grimacing smiles because they told themselves that Cilydd was having some sort of relapse – reacting to what happened to him all those years ago. It's a phase, they told themselves.

But then it came – the inevitable weekend when he would be completely, utterly alone. Gwelw was off to an orthopaedic conference; Lleuwen going with her college friends to a spa hotel. There was no question of him going with either of them, though he tried his best to argue a case for it.

'Orthopaedic conferences are the dryest, most boring things, Cilydd, you just wouldn't have the foggiest what everyone was going on about. Trust me, you wouldn't enjoy it,' Gwelw said, before clipping her briefcase firmly shut, cracking – or so it felt to Cilydd – every one of his bones as she did so.

'Dad, there's no way you're coming with me. The idea of you lurking around the pool in your bathrobe watching us, it's just... creepy,' Lleuwen said. 'Mum, tell him it's weird.'

'Cilydd, she's right, it's weird. This has got to stop now. The girls are in their twenties, they don't need a chaperone. You have to have your own life. Haven't you got any losses to adjust?'

Cilydd could not shake the feeling that something truly terrible was about to happen to him, and that if he let his wife and daughter walk out of the house that weekend, he was unlikely ever to see them again. He resorted to begging them to stay. He found himself on the driveway taking his wife's bags back out of the car.

'Cilydd, for God's sake, leave them where they are,' she said. Even when she was angry she would not raise her voice; her teeth would form a dam, holding her fury in place with perfect stillness. 'People are looking.'

Out of the corner of his eye he saw some brown curtains rustling in the house opposite. He wondered who else was watching them.

'Back they go. That's it. Good. Thank you. Now,' she said, as though addressing a small child. 'You stay here. Have a weekend on your own. Maybe it'll do you good. And don't give Lleuwen any grief when she leaves.'

'But really now...'

'*Cariad...*' his wife said, finitely, with a hard-hitting c. You knew when she said *cariad*, an unusual departure from her ivory-solid expressions, she meant business. As she drove away he waved limply at her, noticing that she wasn't even looking in her rear-view mirror at him – she was merely observing the road – in keeping with her correctness, her precision, her attention to rules and regulations. When his daughter left three hours later, he tried to restrain himself from going downstairs. Instead he watched her getting into her friend's car from an upstairs window, and stopped his knuckles from rapping out a desperate farewell.

By the time she'd rounded the corner the phone was ringing.

The first night without them was bearable, just about, though he could not shake the feeling that someone, somewhere, knew all about him and Doged, someone who was waiting for an opportune moment to bring his world crashing down at his feet. In a fit of paranoia he bolted every door in the house, and took the phone off the hook. Then he thought of his wife and Lleuwen, of how they would be trying to get in touch with him, perhaps, to see how he was. He imagined how selfish and stupid he would look if they arrived home, thinking he had done himself harm, only to find him sitting in his chair, watching the television, and so he put the phone back. He sat there, perfectly still, just watching it – as if observing a creature in the wild. The moment he let his shoulders relax and eyes wander, it started ringing. It knew, he thought. The telephone knew and it was going to devour him whole if he moved. And so he held his breath and ignored it. The seventh time it rang he thought it had to be Gwelw, and so he took his chances. It was. She wanted to know why he wasn't answering. 'Didn't hear it ring,' he lied. 'A technical fault, the email's down as well, I'll get someone to look at it tomorrow. How are things at the conference?' he added, affecting a jovial tone that was completely at odds with his churning insides. 'It's OK,' said Gwelw, 'the same old chitter-chatter about bones.' She launched into something he didn't understand about new research in osteochondritis dissecans, and some peculiarities of the femoral head in recent cases of dislocation. As usual he bumbled his way through the conversation, half-listening, thinking that Femoral Head sounded like a nice place to go for a picnic. All the time she was talking he could only think of what kind of intellectual, informed input Doged would have offered. Doged, from what he could gather, had been a fierce intellect. Good old reliable Doged. The only unreliable thing he had ever done – so everyone though – was kill himself. Thinking about it now, even tumbling upside down in the air he had looked curiously upright.

He poured himself a glass of wine and switched on the television to watch the news. Then he wished he hadn't. A familiar face flashed up on the screen. A body had been found a few miles south – that of a young man in his twenties. It was one of the faces from the network – a face that Cilydd himself had scanned in. He remembered being unnerved by that particular face – the boy had looked troubled. Ffercos son of Poch, flashed the news bulletin. Even the name sounded aggressive, like a pitchfork through the eye. Now he'd been found in a ditch, face down, with bite marks all over his body. It appeared he'd been attacked by some creature; perhaps a wild cat, the reporter speculated. Poch – a man he'd spoken to on several occasions – appeared briefly to read a statement on behalf of the family. It spoke of their relief that their son had been returned to them. But the whole thing made no sense. Ffercos had been missing for years, but the pathologist's report showed that he had only recently been killed.

Cilydd turned off the light and sat in the dark. He

breathed deeply, and tried to find stillness within himself. The news item had given him perspective. The telephone, he thought, in itself, had no power to harm him. Even a voice at the other end, he reasoned, was just a voice, a tinny little thing with no authority.

A knock at the window was something else.

This – accompanied by a white hand on a pane of glass, which retreated into the darkness almost as soon as it had appeared – was something he could not very well ignore. The knock came again, then there was the sound of crunching gravel, as the owner of that hand apparently hurried along to the back of the house with stalking, confident footsteps. Next came an eye, pressed to the glass door – seeking him out in the darkness of the hallway. He stood there suspended, frozen, watching the shimmer of a stranger staring in at him.

'Is it about Doged?' he ventured. 'It's about Doged, isn't it?'

No one spoke. The figure put a hand on the wall, leaning slightly sideways.

'It might be,' came the voice. Lighter, more boyish than it had sounded on the phone. Unserious almost. Not a voice to be terrified of, somehow.

There was nothing for it but to get rid of the pane of glass standing between him and his past. He surprised himself by the steadiness of his hands as he unbolted every single lock, letting the door swing open, revealing a figure standing in the white pool of the security light. The boy in front of him, red haired, standing a little askew, perhaps in shyness, perhaps in mockery of him – had a face which unnerved him. The similarity was uncanny.

'Aren't you going to ask me in, then?' he said, impatiently. 'Nice picture,' he then added, looking beyond Cilydd to the portait of himself, Gwelw and Lleuwen mounted on the wall. The resentment flickered at the corners of his all-too-familiar mouth.

'Are you… are you… you can't surely be...' his heart was pounding now, banging out strange rhythms. My heart knows him, he thought – it *is* him.

'Is it you who's been ringing?' he asked.

'Can I come in? I can tell you more once I'm inside. I don't like being outside.' The boy's tone was impossible to detect – one minute it seemed thick with condescension, the next minute, thin with naivety. A little boy who did not like being left outside.

'Before you come in I think you should know that Doged's death was nothing to do with me,' Cilydd blurted out, 'and I'm not in the habit of inviting strangers into my house.'

The word 'stranger' stood between them, blocking the entrance to Cilydd's home. It came out too quickly, and he regretted saying it. And yet, this boy was a stranger. He knew that what he saw in front of him was Goleuddydd's head on a young man's shoulders, with his own ears appearing as an awkward appendage on either side, but the strangeness, the distance between them, was there all the same.

'If you let me in I'll explain it all. You know who I am, don't you?'

In all the times Cilydd had envisaged this happening it had never been like this. Once the boy had entered his home, it seemed that words merely evaporated into the fraught air between them. There were too many questions for Cilydd even to begin asking, and fifteen years' worth of history lurking on the boy's tongue which Cilydd, for some reason, wanted to keep at bay. It all seemed too much. And so Cilydd kept conversation to a minimum. He merely asked the boy if he would like something to eat, for he looked hungry, and then asked him if he would like to lie down. He looked as though he had been walking for miles, his hair was ruffled and dirty, and his eyelids drooped. He watched him – his son, the stranger – devouring a ham and cheese sandwich, and scrutinised every single munch and grab and grunt and fidget to see if there were traces of himself in there anywhere, (and still he saw nothing but those ears), and then took him to the spare bedroom and let him lie for a while. He kept the door ajar – mainly to reassure himself that what was happening was not just a figment of his imagination. Creeping silently to the door every now and then he watched the rise and fall of that pale, adolescent chest, and knew with certainty that this was his son.

A little while later they met, awkwardly, on the landing. Cilydd had been pacing back and forth on the same patch of carpet for what seemed like days. It was the boy who spoke first.

'Thanks for the room,' the boy said.

'A room is not a house,' Cilydd said, recalling a line from a song he'd heard many years ago. 'And a house is not a home...' Cilydd realised too late that he was mildly hysterical now, that the situation had thrown him out of himself, into some parody of the man he once knew.

The boy looked at him and smiled uncertainly.

'Do you always talk like that?'

'Like what?'

'Like you're rehearsing or something.'

'Yes, I suppose I do,' he replied, thinking how unrehearsed he was for this particular performance. The boy's face remained serious, unruffled by expression. 'Do you have a name?' He tried to recall which names he and Goleuddydd had discussed. He had liked simple, old-fashioned things: Alys, Gwen, Cadi for a girl; Tomos, Huw, Rhys for a boy. Goleuddydd, of course, wanted something more eccentric, something she could lay claim to. Splitting her own name in half like a fortune cookie she'd said, how about Dydd, *Cilydd?* A child that was perpetually a new day. Or Golau, a shining beacon of a baby. And yet no matter how many times they'd discussed it, that little thing that was furling inside her had always been nameless.

'Culhwch,' the boy said. 'My name's Culhwch because I was born in a...'

'Oh, God,' Cilydd said, cupping his face in his hands. 'Yes, I do know where you were born. That much I do know.'

Cilydd found himself returning on his hands and knees again to the globular dark of the pigsty. Cul-hwch. A name even Goleuddydd couldn't have conjured up. The pig-run. Pig boy. A detestable name; forever binding the boy to the awful fate of his birth. 'But where have you... I mean what have you...' his voice was trembling now, and he realised, too late, that he was about to cry. When it came there was no stopping it. It seemed that it gushed forth from a place that had been holed up for years and years, and there was so much water there; muggy, stagnant, stinking, that he couldn't stop until it had all come out.

When he looked up, the boy was looking down at him, consolingly. Suddenly he was the little boy; this man his father.

'I know this must be terribly difficult for you,' he said, laying his arm on Cilydd's shoulder. 'I'm really very sorry about the phone calls. I hadn't meant it to start like that. But you see, it's just something I happened across and I thought...' He stopped in his tracks and took his arm away, as though it had wandered there on its own and needed to be retrieved. 'Let's just say I thought it best that I had something over you.'

'I didn't kill Doged,' Cilydd said. He said it firmly and surprised himself by how much he actually believed it. He hadn't killed Doged.

'I'm sure you didn't. And the person who thinks you did is probably mistaken. But I need your help. And I wasn't going to take any chances. I suppose it's possible, isn't it, that you will help me anyway. Will you, help me?'

'I'll help you as much as I can. But you have to tell me where you've been. We have to sit down and try to make sense of it all. There's so much to get through, isn't there. And I suppose we'll have to inform the police and...'

'No,' said the boy, slightly panicked. 'Not the police.'

'But we have to, you've been missing for... for years and it's our duty to...'

'There's another duty I'm obliged to fulfil first. Please. You have to help me. Not the police. Not yet.'

As he looked at the boy, tracing once more the familiar curve of flesh around the mouth and nose, something like calmness enveloped him. He couldn't fathom it – right now he should have been panicked, stressed, grappling with the phone, dialling emergency numbers. Shaking his son by the shoulders, mopping up the last of his grief with the sleeve of his dressing gown. But he wanted to do none of those things. The boy had convinced him, just by being here, that the best thing to do was nothing. Just keep looking at one another, take every new, surprising moment as it came.

'OK,' he said. 'No police. But you have to tell me what happened to you. You have to understand that this is a shock. I'd given up on you. You do realise that. I thought you were dead. Please just tell me what you know. Who were your abductors? Were they... I hope they were kind to you.'

'I'll tell you everything when we get to Arthur's house,' the boy said.

'Arthur? What's Arthur got to do with this?'

'He's got everything to do with it. He's the one who found me.'

'Arthur's never found anybody in his life.'

The boy smiled. Even the crooked teeth were Goleuddydd's; a bridge of imperfection across a cavernous mouth.

'Oh, he doesn't know it yet.'

'But... look, Culhwch, I think this is all moving a little too quickly...'

'Not quickly enough,' the boy said, looking at his watch. 'We have to go now. Right now. You said you'd help me. So let's go.'

'What do you mean, go? Go where?'

'To Arthur's house...'

'But it's, it's past midnight and....'

'Arthur will be up, won't he?' said the boy knowingly. 'Arthur's always up. Come on.'

The boy tugged him lightly on his sleeve and it seemed that this was all it took – a gentle gesture from the son he'd been looking for most of his life and he was out in the thick of night, driving into the unknown in silence.

Culhwch seemed to know exactly where the flat was, walking a few paces ahead of him down the street. Little flaws jumped out at Cilydd. A tiny little scar on his son's forehead. A chicken-pox pot hole on his cheek. A scratch dulling on his left eyelid. Imprints from the life he had lived up till now; falls, grazes, illnesses his father hadn't been there to witness. A whole history of happenings, furrowed in flesh.

Arthur took his time. Cilydd heard him stumble down the stairway, working his way through the forest of Post-it leaves to get to the front door. How much would Culhwch tell Arthur? He wondered whether the whole nasty business with Doged would have to come up.

His cousin opened the door wearing only his boxer shorts and a T-shirt, clutching a glass of whisky in one hand and a pen in the other. Insomnia lurked in his irises.

'Cilydd,' he said, wearing a faint look of amusement. 'Who's your little friend?'

'Who do you think? It's him. He's come back,' he replied, letting the information hang in the air between them. He thought of the fifteen long years that had passed since he and Arthur sat hunched over his desk, going over and over the details of Goleuddydd's disappearance.

'Who's come back?' Arthur asked.

'My son,' he said, although even in saying it he felt

ridiculous, a sham of a father who hadn't even been there to nurse his son through chicken pox.

Arthur stared at the boy, before walking right up to him and tracing his nose with his fingers, as if trying to work out whether what he saw before him was real.

'My God... I've never, never been so right about anything before,' he said, breathlessly.

'You're quite the artist,' his son said.

'What do you mean? What are you both talking about?' Cilydd was starting to get angry now. Already his son – his rare find on this fateful night – seemed to be falling out of his grasp.

Culhwch walked past them both and climbed the stairs. Watching him disappearing onto the landing Cilydd instinctively followed – he knew how easy it was to lose someone; that they were always a split second away from disappearing. He was afraid Arthur's house and all its paraphernalia would swallow this boy up and they would have to start all over again. Arthur pulled him back.

'Don't be angry with me, Cilydd. All I did was

refuse to give up, that's all. You know most private eyes give up on a case after two to five years. They terminate their contracts. But not me. Not this time. In the absence of a body, there is always hope. And this just proves that I was right. He was out there, wasn't he?'

'What exactly did you do?'

'I think it's easier if I show you.'

Culhwch, it seemed, was one step ahead of them. He stood in the doorway of Arthur's study, his arms folded, contemplating what he saw inside.

'Go ahead,' Arthur urged. 'Take a look.'

What Cilydd saw next left him reeling. The walls were covered in various sketches – all, it seemed, of his son at different phases in his life. There was one of him as a baby, one of him as a nine-year-old boy, one of him on the brink of adolescence. And one which exactly mirrored the way he looked now.

'You're good,' said Culhwch. 'You're really good. I mean, it's pure guesswork as far as I can see. But somehow, you knew what combination I was going to be. Of my mother and father. Didn't you?'

'I used to do hundreds of these things, sitting in the town square. Parents would come, wanting pictures of their children. The likeness was always easy for me, so I never even had to really concentrate when I was sketching – but one thing I always did notice was the similarity to the mother in every single child, even the boys. The mother would always be there, dawdling about, doing other things, maybe looking after other children, and it was always the dad – the proud dad – that would be standing over me, watching me do it, looking for himself in there somewhere. And I'd just stare at the mother and stare at the child and would see it all in there – maybe not in an obvious way, but hidden in little pockets of flesh, little mannerisms, little expressions that were the mother's alone. And if the mother was of a certain ilk – I mean if the mother had presence, and we both know, Cilydd, what *presence* she had, what a fireball she was – then you could guarantee that it would be in the child, too. A magic touch of flesh, holding all the features together.'

Arthur was right of course – whatever inexplicable, potent thing Goleuddydd had had, this boy had it too, and he sat there, emanating it, oozing her iridescence all over the place. His son stared on at sketches of himself as a toddler. Arthur had been inventive in his artistry – it showed the boy engaged in all sorts of infantile activities. Holding a beaker, munching on a banana, things which may or may not have happened, but which were, angle by angle, stroke by stroke, handing fragments of his son's stolen history back to his father.

'After you stopped working for the network I began posting these pictures up, attached to your son's profile. I knew you wouldn't have liked me doing it, so I didn't tell you. I remember you saying once that you could never create a likeness of someone who's never existed. I suppose it posed a challenge to me when you said that – so I defied you. That is how you found us, isn't it?'

They both turned to look at Culhwch.

'It took me a while, you understand, to know that I was a missing person in the first place. But once I knew it, things came together. And if it wasn't for Arthur's work I'd never have known that profile was mine. I had no name, no identity. I was nothing. Until those pictures appeared there. And when I was ready to go searching for myself, well, it was easy. There I was. And there was my mother. And there was every thing I needed. Even down to the addresses and... and the phone numbers.'

At that point he avoided Cilydd's gaze. Cilydd recalled the blank profile – the hateful question mark. He hated the implication that he'd given up on his son; that he'd allowed him to become a non-entity, a nothing, as he put it. It was only Arthur who'd been brave enough to give him a face, to illuminate him, to let him pierce through the darkness to arrive back where he belonged.

It was almost as if Arthur had sketched him into being.

Culhwch

Culhwch told them he was brought up on a small-holding on the edge of a large forest. From when he was a child his parents had insisted the forest held unknown dangers, he would be swallowed up by it, engulfed by the greenery, they said. He was home schooled – something he never challenged, for his mother told him that this was what happened when you were exceptionally bright – and they lived without a television, a computer, without any form of news from the outside world. It was merely the way of things. Occasionally some other adults would come over for a day out – friends of his parents. Although he never saw them arrive he knew, somehow, that they had come through the forest. They were an odd bunch, too, of all ages, all looking peculiarly pale and gaunt. None of them had children. But they would play with him, and this was compensation enough. Swinging on a rope amidst haystacks, running through the fields, hiding in bushes; laughing – it was a rare rush of activity and happiness which left him elated for days. There was very little laughter at home – and he felt it was somehow inside him, this laughter, a natural part of him, an impulse which was never fully satisfied. But even as he laughed, he was aware of his unsmiling parents lurking behind him, two shadows that were always hovering on the periphery of his life, as though they were nervous about what such laughter could bring.

His parents slept in separate rooms. When he was a little boy, he used to dream of having a family where everyone huddled up in bed together, like they did in his books. When he asked his mother about it she would say something about 'special' children having 'special' parents – and that one day he would understand why things had to be like this. One day, she said, they would explain everything.

On the farm they bred only birds – there were no livestock, bar the ones he saw dotted on the faraway hillside. There were several aviaries in the back garden, and a huge, empty pigsty in the yard. The pigsty became his den – he would sit in there for hours on end and play out his fantasy of being a swineherd, with real swine to look after. He was never let near the birds. He was faintly aware of them, just sitting there, beyond the mesh, hardly moving at all. Every now and then the birds would be sold off – leaving the smallholding eerily empty. On those days he snuck into one of the aviaries, hoping to collect a few mementoes. But there was never any trace of those birds. No scent, not so much as a tiny feather.

Once a new batch of birds arrived, he would watch his father transferring them from the cages into the aviary. Birds were squawking, active creatures – so he thought from his books – and yet these birds would sit entirely still on their perches while they were moved about, their feathers hardly ruffling at all. When they flew they simply slid into the air, as though easing themselves into some glutinous substance, opening their beaks as though drinking it in. The only moving part of them seemed to be their restless orange eyes – which followed you wherever you went. They were beautiful, too, like no other birds he'd seen – their coats velvety blue, with a green sheen, and their beaks mustard yellow. He'd never seen them eat anything, and so one day, when his father's back was turned, he fished a piece of bread out of his pocket and held it up to the mesh. To his surprise, the aviary erupted – a volcano of feathers tumbled down upon him, and he felt the sharp sting of beaks as the bread was wrenched from his hand. At that point he remembered his father shouting at him: 'What have you done? Oh Culhwch! What have you done!' He was sent to bed without supper, and the next day the aviary was completely empty. Neither his mother nor his father ever commented on the event but within a few days a fence had been put up around the aviaries so that he couldn't get to them. He hovered outside them often, but never heard a peep from those birds ever again.

Years passed by; the birds and strange, random visitors came and went. He learned about places in the world in his geography lessons yet his mother insisted that you had to cross the forest to get to them. Then, something surprising happened. A few months ago, a few days after his fifteenth birthday, a girl arrived in the house. There was commotion in the thick of night, and he listened to the whole exchange through a crack in the kitchen door. A booming male voice instructed his parents to keep the girl for a few months, while things 'settled down'. He heard his mother saying that one child was enough, with all the birds to care for too – she would not be able to do it. The man retaliated by saying that he had the power to take the boy away if they did not do as he asked. 'Remember, as far as the rest of the world is concerned, he's still missing,' he heard him say, before adding, in a gentler voice: 'Look at her, she'll be no trouble, she never has been. Until now. You owe me this much. I haven't forgotten what you did. You still haven't been forgiven for it.' Through the narrow slit Culhwch could not see the girl properly – but he somehow developed a sense of her – a restless, moving thing under the man's grasp, there was a kind of white dazzle about her, bright blonde hair and pale toes.

For fear of getting caught he went back to bed, thinking he'd be offered an explanation the next day. But at the breakfast table there was no mention of the previous night's escapade. His mother sipped her juice gravely, his father shoved little hummocks of cereal into his mouth; neither one of them said a word. There was simply no trace of the girl; not so much as a stray hair on the kitchen floor. It was the first time Culhwch realised that the world in which he lived was somehow not real at all.

Days passed, and life carried on as normal. And yet, everything seemed to have changed. There was – he could not really explain it – a new energy in the house. White flowers sprung up in the garden, and the patches of damp that had been collecting on the bathroom ceiling suddenly receded. There was a new lightness and freshness about the place. He knew the girl could not be far.

One morning, when his father had fallen asleep in his chair, he followed his mother on her morning stroll. To his surprise, she entered the forest. He waited a while before entering himself, remembering his mother's warning. But soon enough he found himself following her footsteps through the wilderness, which was easier than he'd anticipated, for every few steps he noticed a curious little hollow in the soil, as though something had been uprooted. This dark trail led him to a clearing in the woods, where he came upon a small hut perched on the edge of a stream. There, he saw his mother, kneeling on the muddy bank, sleeves rolled up, pouring a bucket of water over the head of a naked young girl, gently washing her hair. There was such tenderness between them, even as his mother sighed and puffed and pretended to find the whole thing bothersome, he saw that she enjoyed it, that the girl's presence was a joy to her. She shampooed the hair as though it were fine silk between her fingers – and the girl, muted, frightened-looking as she was, yielded her head to his mother's hands and gave into the caress. It wasn't until the girl got up and stood there, illuminated in the sun's rays that Culhwch saw how truly beautiful she was. He had never seen anybody's naked body except for his own before, and it seemed to him the most wondrous, the most pure thing he had seen. And yet there was something odd about the body, something imbalanced, which he couldn't put his finger on. She did not look like the girls in his books.

The moment his mother stepped back from the water, she seemed to harden, taking the girl by the hand and roughly shoving her back into the hut. As she turned away to lock the door, Culhwch saw his chance and made a run for it back to the house. He arrived just as his father was waking up, and pretended he'd been reading in his room. When his mother came back he could not resist the temptation of asking her how her walk had been. 'Oh lovely,' she said. 'Such lovely flowers springing up at this time of year.'

He snuck out that night, following the moon's path through the wilderness until he came to the hut. As he walked he had the feeling that someone was watching him, but when he turned back there was no one there. He carried on. Still the feeling persisted, and slowly he began to realise that the watchers were above him. When he looked up, there they were – the birds. Around a dozen of them, silently flitting from branch to branch, moving as he moved, stopping when he stopped. He wondered if his mother knew they were out. It wasn't until he reached the hut that they descended, perching themselves on the wooden porch, a barricade of orange eyes. And yet, when he moved, they shuffled sideways to let him pass. He knocked at the door. No whimpering came from inside, just a small, quiet voice, asking him what he wanted. Within a few moments her face appeared at the mesh window. He could only see her hair, shining white in the moonlight, dazzling him. The door was bolted shut. He told her he wanted to help.

'You can't help someone who doesn't exist,' she said. 'There's no point in freeing me. Who would have me?'

A bird hopped up beside him, scratching the mesh with a sharp claw. He thought he detected a faint smile from her at that moment. She raised her own pale palm to the window as a greeting.

'Hello you,' she said to the bird, in lilting tones, so unlike the tired voice he had just heard.

'I've never seen the birds out,' he said. 'My mother would never let them out this far.'

'Oh, don't you worry about them. They can look after themselves. Can't you?'

The bird squawked – the first time Culhwch had ever heard one of them make a sound. It was curious, somehow melodic and off-key at the same time. He tried to touch the bird but it hobbled away from him, keeping its eyes fixed on the shadow behind the door.1qa

That's when he asked her who she was. He asked her for a name.

'A name... is about the only thing I have got,' she said. 'My name's Olwen.'

Olwen. A white trail. He thought of the damp receding, of the flowers rising like bold sails from the ground. So it was her, sweeping her whiteness over their lives.

'But why are you here?' he asked. 'Why are you with us?'

'My father, Ysbaddaden, sent me away. He's going to do something awful while I'm gone, I know it. I'll be going back to him once it's over.'

He asked her what she had done to make her father want to send her away. She would not tell him. She asked him who he was.

'The son of the woman who locked you up.'

She asked him if he was sure. He'd never thought about it until that moment.

'Because I think... I think you might be the one... the one left over. They made a mess of things so they had to send you away. Otherwise, you might, might have been me. But you're not me. I'm me. Though it doesn't feel like it sometimes. All I know is... I don't think you are their son.'

The moment she said it he began to feel funny. His chest constricted, his eyes suddenly began to droop and his whole body felt as though it would slump to the floor. A grey haze began to settle over his mind. It was as though the truth had winded him. 'Oh,' she said, seeing him grab the wall of the hut for support. 'Oh no. You have to go. Quickly – before it takes hold.'

'Before what takes hold?' he asked her.

'Please, go now,' she said.

There was such urgency in her voice at that moment that he had no choice but to listen to her. He struggled for breath in the dark, turned on his heels and trudged slowly back through the forest, back to the farm, to certainty, to order. The closer he got to the smallholding the more the heaviness lifted, his legs became his own again, his eyelids sprung open. Even without looking up he knew the birds were not with him now; that he had only been a means of leading them to her. In the distance he heard that one faint squawk swell into bright, triumphant chatter.

By the time he was back in his own bed, his head was clear once more, and he knew that she was right, he was not their son. Perhaps he had always known.

He waited before going to see her again. His mother came and went, and he dreamt of the damp flaxen hair in that stream, longing to touch it, to see her properly. He thought of nothing but her, this girl in the hut in the forest. And yet his parents acted as though nothing was amiss. He had expected them to find the birds missing on their daily rounds, and yet there was no mention of them at all. The three of them would still sit around that table and pretend their life together was entirely normal and ordinary. As if there was not a girl living a few feet away from them, caged, like the silent birds in the aviary. As though his parents had not done something so terrible that they had to keep looking after her and had little or no say in what they could and could not do.

He was determined to set her free. Grabbing his father's tools the following night, he had never felt such bravado. He would wrench that door open and she would fall into his arms, he envisaged it time and time again. His heart was pounding as he approached the hut. To his surprise the door was wide open. The strip of light from his torch revealed it to be bare and empty. Fury rose up in him; he kicked the door, punched a wall, shouted into the night. He had not been prepared for the physical pain of losing her, and he knew – at that moment – that there was nothing more important to him than finding her again. Once he was able to still himself, he lay down on the wooden floor, frantically sniffing the air for any trace of her. That's when he became aware of a silhouette in the doorframe, one that was all too familiar. His mother.

'What are you doing here, Culhwch?' she asked. He could hear the fear in her voice. 'What have we told you about the forest?'

'You've told me a lot of things,' he said, without getting up. 'None of them seem to be true.'

'I think we'd better go back to the house,' his mother said. 'We can talk things through. Perhaps we could answer any questions you may have. It isn't... we aren't... we aren't bad people, me and your dad. It's just we got... a bit caught up in some things and...'

'But you're not my parents, are you?' he said. The sentence surfaced in the dark between them.

'No,' his mother said quietly. 'No, we're not.'

'What's going on? You always said you would tell me. One day, you said. We'll tell you – you'll understand. We'll explain everything. Isn't that what you said?'

'I always wanted to – it was your father...'

'He's not my father though, is he! Stop pretending.'

'No, he's not. Culhwch, I'm sorry, he's not... he's not... not my husband either. He's nothing to me. This whole thing... it's just not... not real. I'm as tired of it as you are.'

His mother burst into tears. He'd never heard her cry before. He wanted to put an arm over her shoulder, but he stopped himself – holding on with all his might to the anger which rose in him, a new and delicious feeling. He kicked the wall again. Enough to hurt himself. Enough to feel alive.

'What have you done with her, with Olwen?'

'She's gone home, Culhwch, that's all. Let's go back to the house, eh? I'll explain things.'

'Was it the birds?' he asked. 'Did the birds set her free?'

His mother gawped at him, as though he'd said something ridiculous.

'No, Culhwch. God, no. The birds wouldn't be able to come here...'

'Don't lie to me! They were here, I saw them.'

His mother's face paled with shock.

'No, they couldn't have been.'

'They were here, I tell you. They knew her...'

'But that's not possible, I mean they aren't... aren't meant to be anything to do with her... they're... it's hard to explain. Look, let's go back to the house. We'll sit down and talk.'

Culhwch wasn't sure what happened next. It seemed unreal to him, walking back through that forest to a house he had called his home for fifteen years, knowing full well he wasn't supposed to be there. He trailed behind his mother's shadow feeling like a lost little boy once again. But then he saw something. Just as the moon fell away under a cloud and the whole forest became a silvery, slippery pool, the ground suddenly revealed a trail of white flowers, weaving their way through the forest, in the opposite direction. He couldn't explain it but he knew, at that moment, that it was Olwen, that she had left a pathway for him, that she wanted him to find her. He realised suddenly that that's what his mother had uprooted on her journey into the forest, eradicating all traces of life that Olwen had left behind. And so he turned on his heels and ran. The white flowers grew bolder, meatier and brighter as he passed by, the petals spilling over themselves, forming elaborate patterns, boasting new textures. He ran and ran for what seemed like hours, until he came upon an enormous building, right at the far end of the forest. That was where the flowers stopped.

The house was a colossus of white brick. Its blank face stared down at him. The gardens around it were pristine and well kept, and yet the house was eerily quiet, and apparently deserted. But what he saw next stunned him. Looking up to a high window he saw Olwen, face pressed against the glass. Her body was bulging, and he saw now why she had seemed so curiously heavy and lopsided; she was pregnant. He'd never seen a pregnant woman before, though he'd seen pictures of mammals with bulging stomachs. He saw her hand shooing him away, as she turned to talk to someone in the room. The fright in her eyes was unmistakable and her hand was telling him firmly; *go, now.*

He obeyed her gesture, and walked all around the forest until he came to a road. A lovely, plain, forgiving road, that eventually provided him with passing traffic, a kind truck driver, and a means of bringing him to a nearby town. He asked the truck driver if he knew anything about the building in the forest and he said that it was the home of a millionaire.

'He's loaded that guy. Ysbaddaden Bencawr, I think he's called. Acres and acres of land and the tightest security you'll ever get, I reckon. No one's allowed within miles of the place. And rumour has it he lives there all alone too. Deliveries by helicopter, that sort of thing. Stinking rich. No one knows how he made his fortune, but it's got to be something underhand if you ask me. Drugs or something. Coffee beans even. No, probably oil, warfare, something dodgy, it'll be something illicit, you mark my words.'

Ysbaddaden. He remembered the name. Olwen's father. They drove on in silence, the words chiming in Culhwch's mind.

'I don't know who I am. I... I think I belong to someone else,' the boy finally said. 'Can you help me?'

'Hand yourself in,' the truck driver advised. 'Look, I'll take you to the police station. You can tell them everything. They're bound to have some files on you or something.'

He drove Culhwch to the police station. He said he'd wait for him. Culhwch went in, saw all these people in uniforms, drunk people being shoved about, girls shouting and crying. He thought of his mother, that frail little bird, being caged in such a place, and he retreated. The truck driver, fiddling with his iPhone, looked up at him excitedly.

'I just googled something,' he said. 'You know,

just curious like. The Missing Persons' Network, it's called. And I found… I think I found you!'

That's when Arthur's sketch came up. With Cilydd's details, phone number, address. Attached were the news items about Goleuddydd's disappearance and murder. Culhwch couldn't believe it had been that easy – he had never seen such a contraption as an iPhone, a tiny little screen in his hand which showed him a portrait of himself, sketched by someone who had never seen him. His own history, which had been kept from him for fifteen years, was something that could be clicked upon by a stranger in seconds. He read his whole sorry story beneath a fug of fingertips. The truck driver dropped him off in front of Cilydd's house – wishing him all the best. All his life he had only been three miles away from his father's home.

But he couldn't go in. Not straight away. It didn't seem right. He saw a woman and a girl coming and going – saw Cilydd himself smiling in the driveway, looking content. So he spent a few weeks in the town thinking things through; sleeping rough, doing a few odd jobs here and there, scrabbling for money. *And making phone calls*, Cilydd thought.

'So here I am, finally,' he said, looking up at Cilydd and Arthur. 'I've wasted enough time, just thinking about things. Now I need to do something. Olwen is probably due any day now. And we've got to help her. That's why I'm here.'

Arthur, still in his boxer shorts, gawped at him. Cilydd did not know what to say. He noticed that Culhwch had said nothing about Doged. Perhaps the boy was biding his time, or had decided to shield Arthur from the truth. Either way, Cilydd was grateful.

'I knew, once I found you, that you'd help me,' said the boy. 'Help me to get Olwen out of Ysbaddaden's house.'

'Ysbaddaden Bencawr. Now there's a name I never thought I'd hear again,' Arthur said, shaking his head. 'You know him?' Culhwch turned to Arthur.

'Know *of* him, yes. Used to be a private eye, of course, back in the day. Always vying for the same cases as I was. Neither of us were particularly successful, of course, as far as I know he never solved a single case either – though I don't suppose it even matters, considering how much money he's got now.' Arthur sighed. 'I guess I drew the short straw.'

'But what does he do? I mean, where does all the money come from? That house, I've never seen anything like it. There must be a hundred bedrooms in that place. And it's just him and Olwen, isn't it?'

'Funny – I never heard he had a daughter. Rumour had it that he lived there all alone. I mean, that's how the rest of us private eyes always comforted ourselves about the whole thing – ah, yes, Ysbaddaden, he's a millionaire but has he got anyone to share it with? No. Living all alone in that house. Better a pauper than a lonely man.'

Culhwch's eyes circled the room.

'Don't you live alone?'

'Yes...' Arthur looked away. 'But that's beside the point. I heard the money was some inheritance. A bit of luck, I think.'

'Well, we need to get Olwen away from him,'

Culhwch said. 'And we need to do it quickly. I've got a feeling that if we don't get her out of there soon that something awful will happen to her. That's why I need your help. Both of you. I have to find her. I can't explain to you what it means to me. If we find her then everything will be OK. I mean, it's hard enough to make sense of it all but if we just find her then maybe some good can come of all this. I mean, this girl. I love her... I know it sounds stupid and you probably think I'm just a child, but I do, I really do. Look, all I need is some transport. Just to get to Ysbaddaden's estate. Ysbaddaden Bencawr has got something to do with my disappearance, I know he has. He has something over my parents; that's why my mother was looking after Olwen. Possibly it's why they were looking after me, too. And if we go to him, we can find out what is going on. Don't you want to know what happened to me? Why I was taken?'

'Of course we do,' said Arthur, 'don't we Cilydd?'

Cilydd said he needed a glass of water, and went to the kitchen. Arthur joined him. Cilydd paced the room, peering every now and then through the crack in the door to check his son was still there.

'Well, what do you make of it?' he asked his cousin.

'I don't know. I knew something like this was going to happen soon. I mean, have you been... well, having phone calls?'

'Phone calls? No.' Cilydd lied, feeling the colour drain out of him.

'Well I have, and when I came home yesterday – well, I could swear someone had been in the house. And all day today I've had this restless feeling, like I was waiting for something to happen. So restless, all I could do was get drunk, like I was trying to ward off some terrible feeling. And now, it's gone. Because it's like I've been waiting for him, and now he's here. He's finally here.'

'But is he... I mean, is he who he says he is?'

'There's no doubt, he's your son, Cilydd. I mean, even the ears...'

'I know...' Cilydd said. His son. How simple it sounded; though how utterly complex. 'But, I mean, living on that farm, all those years – that farm, of all places! It's the farm where they found her body, isn't it? It doesn't make any sense. Surely the police checked everything – how could he have been under our noses, all those years? I remember them saying that a family had moved in... but surely...'

'The police, Cilydd – you can never rely on the police. I told you that. I mean, they're full of Anlawdd types – full of themselves. That's why you came to me in the first place, remember? I think we should help him Cilydd, and if he's right, about Ysbaddaden, well, I'm not being selfish here, but, it could really be the making of me...'

Arthur grinned, and took a final swig of his whisky.

Before they set out, Culhwch asked them if they would cut his hair. It had grown long and straggly over the years, had come to define him, and he did not want to be recognised when he entered the house. Arthur plugged in his shaver and went about shearing the boy's head. Cilydd sat silently under the naked bulb of Arthur's kitchen and watched Goleuddydd's hair coming off, lock by lock. It was funny how comforting it was to see it, flowing orange all over the floor. The thought that even after you had long left this world something of you, something as essential, as intricate, as your hair, remained, on someone else's scalp. He offered to scoop up the leftovers and found himself looting the lot of it, shoving it into his pocket, where it bristled against his hand, a living, passionate part of someone he'd loved so dearly, come back to him, grown again on the surface of his world.

And so Culhwch, Cilydd and Arthur set out, in the thick of night in Arthur's old carpentry van, to find Olwen, daughter of Ysbaddaden Bencawr. Cilydd could not remember the last time he'd done such a thing; taken off like this. Probably never in his life. It just wasn't something he did. Even before Goleuddydd disappeared he would always tell people where he was going, when he would be back. He suddenly realised that now he was the one who was missing, and that his wife and daughter were going to return home in a few hours to find the house empty. He looked again at the figure sitting behind him. This boy who had not known, until recently, that he was a missing person. How could one not know? Throughout his life he had been nurtured, cared for by people he believed to be his parents – yet all that time he had been a foundling.

After they'd driven a few miles out of town, the dark began to clear, giving way to the first peachy hues of day. Soon they came upon a long, narrow road with towering fir trees on the left-hand side. Cilydd felt the scene to be all too familiar, and he realised that this was where the police had brought him, fifteen years ago. His memory smelt the pigsty, and it made him gag.

'I think we should start from here,' Culhwch said. 'Stop the car.'

They got out of the car. The rows of trees went on for ever it seemed, taunting long bodies, standing in their way.

Culhwch walked on without saying a word. Soon

the three of them found themselves entering the maze of woodland. There was no light at the far end, no certainty of anything but darkness. The further on they went, the more Cilydd found himself wanting to grab hold of his son's hand, to stop him from being enveloped by the blackness, an urge which he forced himself to fight. Culhwch battled his way through the greenery, aimlessly, twisting this way and that. As though fighting the earth that refused to give him answers.

'I don't think this is a good idea,' Cilydd said, stopping suddenly in his tracks. 'I mean, have you got any clue where you're going?'

His son turned around to look at him.

'I know that Ysbaddaden's house can't be far...'

'Yes, but there's no clear pathway here. We could end up walking around in circles. I mean, we probably are walking around in circles already. I just don't think... I don't think this is the right way to go about it. I really don't.'

Culhwch turned to look at him. There was a despondency in his eyes which hurt Cilydd. He saw uncertainty flickering there, just beneath his eye-lashes.

'You don't believe me, do you?' he said. 'Either of you. You're just humouring me.'

'Of course we believe you!' came Arthur's chirpy voice, before slapping a sturdy arm on the boy's shoulder. 'It's just maybe we need a plan.'

'There's no time for a plan... I know that we'll find it. She'll... she'll... help us. Just look. Things are getting lighter. Can't you see it?'

At that moment light seemed to come pouring in through the tops of the trees, from some mysterious sun they couldn't see. Everything seemed brighter, better defined – leaves sharpened, twigs and branches all of a sudden like strong limbs, reaching out to help them. They heard a rustling beneath their feet, as though something was aching in the ground, fisting its way through the mud. That's when it came, suddenly, and without warning; a burst of whiteness. One by one, soft tiny heads emerged – eyeless and startling – a long line of petals creating a pathway for them, illuminating a white trail in the damp earth.

'She's here,' Culhwch said, smiling to himself. Arthur and Cilydd looked at each other. 'Trust me. She knows we're coming. We'll find a way in, she'll make sure of it.'

As though in a trance, they followed the boy as he trailed the flowers, trampling each one underfoot as he went to mark their path. The white, trembling spirals sent them left, then right, then left again, the three of them walking in frantic paces, hurtling through brambles, eyes to the ground, until they felt dizzy. Hours passed. The sun slowly abandoned them. A strange feeling crept over Cilydd. Some weakness, right at the very core of him. He realised he had not eaten or slept for hours. But he wanted his body to keep going. Where were his reserves of energy? Surely his body could keep him awake for a few more hours. When Goleuddydd disappeared he had stayed awake for a week or more, the midnight oil of despair spitting and hissing inside him. He needed strength now, resolve. To show his son he could be strong.

But his legs buckled. He found himself on his

knees, staring up. Arthur's eyes seemed to be sloping too, sliding down his face.

'I don't feel too well,' Cilydd said, leaning against a tree to catch his breath.

The hard earth had never felt so comforting, so secure, like a good orthopaedic bed. He slumped at the foot of a tree. The forest seemed to be growing thicker, denser with every passing moment; it seemed additional leaves were flocking to the trees. He squinted up at them. It took him a few moments to see that they were not in fact leaves at all; they were birds. Lithe little leaf-shaped birds, flocking to the branches, all utterly silent.

'Where are they all coming from?' he asked Arthur, in a voice he no longer recognised as his own; dense and mucous-filled.

'I'm not… I'm not... sure,' Arthur's sentence fell into the earth along with its owner.

'Get up!' he was vaguely aware of his son saying. 'Don't give in to it! Get up!' The voice seemed to be getting further and further away; a voice carried off with the waves of dusk, a little boy lost at sea.

'Come back,' his son seemed to be saying. 'Come back.'

Cilydd's last thought was how much the birds looked like the ones Culhwch had described to him, the ones his mother kept in the aviary at the foot of the garden. When they turned their heads slowly their eyes glistened with copper and their feathers seemed to take on an emerald tinge. The twittering was unbearable: a rush of noise, at turns beautiful and terrible. It started with the opening of a single beak, right above him, and somehow escalated, with another bird, and then another, adding their imperfect melody. When Cilydd looked up it seemed the air was dense with feathers and song and by the time he looked down it seemed the earth had fallen away beneath him and he could do nothing but fall, and give in to its dark embrace.

Ysbaddaden Bencawr

Cilydd was first aware of a single, cool breath on his face. His arms felt light by his side, and his eyelids seemed to blossom gently as they opened. He felt remarkable. Better than he'd felt in years.

'Cilydd,' the breath came again. 'Take your time. Savour the waking up. It's never felt so good, believe you me.'

The room was dimly lit and windowless. Even though his body seemed entirely at peace his mind was unclear, full of noise, full of chatter.

'The birds,' he recalled suddenly.

The figure laughed; a rasping, hollow sound.

'Ah yes, magnificent aren't they? Very rare you understand, and notoriously difficult to breed. But once you've got a good flock of them, they really are the most wonderful creatures. So cheap to keep, too. They don't need any food. What keeps them going is pure, clean air. They just eat it up. They've never known hunger. You feed them anything other than air and they die. Your son, Culhwch, killed off a whole batch of them once. Not that I'll hold that against him now – he was just a boy back then. He's had enough to contend with over the years, hasn't he? But let's not talk about him. Let's talk about you. What do you remember, Cilydd, after being in the forest?'

Cilydd's mind was entirely blank. He had no recollection of anything beyond the wild chatter, the crazed weaving of branches above him.

'Nothing, am I right?' came the voice again. 'You remember nothing because you were sleeping – soundly – the kind of sleep most of us can only dream of. Can't imagine you've had much quality sleep in recent years, Cilydd, what with all the drama you've had. Missing wife, missing son – and then all that nasty business with Doged. That's got to be a few years of tossing and turning. That's why I thought I'd give you a break. A good old sleep, courtesy of Rhiannon's Birds. Quite rare, you know, as I said. You can't get them in this country now, of course, seems they all flocked way from here in search of warmer climates – don't blame them personally – but it's here that they belong, so I took it upon myself to start bringing them back. It's amazing how well preserved they are. And how powerful. In ancient times it was thought that they could wake the dead – not that I've witnessed it myself, of course. But they can still lull the living to sleep. Like nobody's business. Once that chattering starts, even the lightest sleepers are off – just like that. Out like a light, as they say.'

The figure scraped a chair across the floor and sat down opposite him. Cilydd's vision was still fuzzy. All he could make out were silvery little peaks of stubble on the man's chin.

'Finding them was rather a piece of good luck. I mean, I was doing quite well without them, getting plenty of business – but having them at my disposal, well, it really gave the business the edge I was looking for. It made every case so much more *interesting*. They're very faithful creatures you see. Not like that wild boar of mine – he'll hunt anyone down, even his own leader, if things get bad. No, these creatures aren't primitive, far from it. They're dignified; refined even. They'll do anything to please their leader, anything. So anything I wanted – I got. No matter how difficult, they helped me obtain it. Look at your wife's case, for example. Never would have managed that one in previous years. But once I had the birds, anything was possible.'

His wife. The words seemed alien to him for a second – wholly separate, floating meaninglessly in the air. Then he felt it. The grief. Dark and sepulchral like a pigsty, right at the core of him.

'You... you abducted my wife?' Cilydd again tried to move out of his chair but something was keeping him there, he couldn't understand what. There were no ropes tying him down. No shackles around his feet. It seemed that he himself was the barrier. The figure laughed. The face fell forward into a ray of light. The man was middle-aged and good-looking, wearing a dark suit that you could tell was expensive, from the way it glided over him, creaseless at every turn.

'Abduction, honestly,' said the man. 'We don't use that vulgar term in here. We don't abduct. We assist. Not that we were able to offer much assistance in her case. It was irresponsible of me to take on a pregnant woman, I can see that now. Not only a pregnant woman but one who was so, how shall we say... *spirited*. I mean, you only had to take one look at her and you knew there would be all sorts of problems. There was no certainty that she'd play ball. But then, everyone thought it was plausible. A new string to our bow, they said – a child. Having a child at our disposal – if you pardon the term – well, it did actually seem somewhat of an... an opportunity.'

Child. Whose child? His history seemed to fragment in his mind. Did he have a son? Then he saw a face. A young man's face. And his mind replayed, with perfect clarity, a door opening to reveal a boy standing in front of him.

'He was my boy,' Cilydd said, remembering the

shock of that moment. The indignation rose in his throat, thickening his voice. 'That's right. He was always my boy. Never anyone else's. He was mine and hers. You had no right to take him.'

'It's not our job to make decisions about the rights and wrongs of any particular case, you understand. We're not here to judge. We must go with what the client wants. That's what we were doing, every step of the way. The contract Goleuddydd signed stipulated quite clearly that she wanted to disappear. That the boy would be ours, to do with as we wished. That's what she wanted. At least... at first.'

'At first?'

'Well, yes. Come on, Cilydd. You know what she was like. She was fine until she got here. We had everything set up – two doctors at the ready to deliver the baby, a nice comfortable room – we even had a birthing ball. She was rolling around on that thing for days. That's when, I think, the whole reality of the situation dawned on her. Too much time to think, you see Cilydd – it will happen when a woman's overdue. And that's when it all went wrong.

That's when we had to rethink the whole thing. And that's when we made our mistakes. And for those we're sorry. We hope they can be put right.'

Cilydd was listening but the words seemed indistinct, floating above him, just like the birds he'd seen a few hours – or was it days – ago. The words would not fly together. Nothing made sense to him.

'Beautiful woman, that wife of yours,' the man continued. 'That red hair, that *chutzpah* of hers. You will recall how she charmed people – that flick of hair, those almond eyes. I should have seen the chaos she would bring, but I couldn't see past *her*. If I'd had my wits about me that day I would have stuck to my guns and I would have told her – it's strictly a one-person business, disappearing. No point bringing a second person into it – no matter how little, how vulnerable they are.'

Vulnerable. The all-too-familiar word came at Cilydd again, slicing his insides. He saw the headlines, the news bulletins. His whole history boomed, as if announced on a supermarket loudspeaker. *The supermarket*, he thought. Oh God, the supermarket.

'You're not saying that she... she knew what she was doing that day? She knew you'd come for her? She wouldn't have done that. She couldn't have.'

'The supermarket was her choice, not ours. The option of choosing how you disappear is still quite new in this operation, you see. But we realised after a few of those boating accidents and nightclub mysteries that we were going to have to keep things varied. I mean, we can't have people making connections. Like your cousin Arthur, for example. People like that are going to burrow away at something until they get to the bottom of it – that's why we have to fox them. People have two choices. They can either select what we term as a *rational disappearance package* – that is, make their feelings of depression known for a few days to friends and family, do a few things that are out of character so that people start to suspect something isn't right, and get that terrible feeling of foreboding that something is about to happen – and then go out in a boat or for a long walk on a cliff and seem to fall off the face of the earth – or they can choose an *irrational disappearance package*, like your wife did and – bam! – they're gone, in one moment, during an ordinary routine day, leaving everybody mystified. And I have to say, Cilydd, Goleuddydd really wanted to play with you. It was a tricky one for us too, what with the security cameras and the like – but we do like a challenge. That's where the birds came in handy. We hadn't used them much before-hand so it was a real risk for us – but, once they were in the supermarket, it worked like a dream. The shoppers dropped like dominoes, aisle by aisle. Goleuddydd wanted to take your glasses. I made her give them back. 'But it's such a tiny detail!' she said. 'Listen here,' I said, 'it's the tiny details that will give the game away. Tiny details build on each other, become huge, colossal, magnificent features. Before long they've got the whole picture.' The only thing I was worried about was the birds – if we'd manage to get them all back into the aviary. But we did, remarkably. Like I told you, they're faithful creatures, they didn't want me to leave without them. They hadn't left a single trace – so we thought – until we saw all the business about the flour aisle on the news.'

Cilydd's mind was racing now. He saw himself wandering about the supermarket, his glasses slightly askew, as she had left them, on his nose.

'She wanted to get away from me,' he said. 'She must have really hated me.'

'Well, it seemed that way, at first, yes. My own diagnosis would be simply a temporary suppression of love caused by hormonal changes. But it may help you to know that once we got her here, once we got her settled in, things started to change. She began – we think – she began pining for you. She changed her mind about the whole operation and wanted out. She wanted to go back. She wanted you to have the baby.'

Of course Goleuddydd would change her mind, Cilydd thought. He knew her better than anyone. Every single thing she did was a whim.

'Then why didn't she come back to me? Why didn't you let her go?'

The man laughed again.

'The contract is very clear. Once you chose to come here, that's it. You can't *reappear*. It would

134

bring the whole operation crashing down around us. You commit to a family here, Cilydd. A family which chooses to live life quietly, away from everything. Which, for some reason or another, does not want to be with their real families, with their so-called loved ones. And why not? We've got everything they need right here. Enough money to pay for everything that's needed, to keep everyone comfortable.'

'So that's how you manage it, then, is it?' Cilydd said bitterly. 'You take money off vulnerable people to fund this place.'

'Come on now, Cilydd. I mean, you're a loss adjustor. You must have seen plenty of people struggling. It's not nice, is it? Here we make sure they're never going to have to struggle again. We do ask for a large sum of money – yes. And most of them find it, even the ones that are worst off. Because it doesn't matter where the money comes from. Once someone has disappeared they're absolved of all their sins and nothing really matters, does it? It's not like they have to pay any of it back to anyone. So people take out loans, get money off their friends. If they really want to come here – let's just say, they find a way. Anyway, I think I've talked enough for now. I think we should go for a little walk, to familiarise you with the place.'

At that point two men entered the room. Two familiar faces.

'Graid son of Eri...' Cilydd said, surprising himself with the memory. He remembered typing this boy's profile as though it were yesterday, except now he wasn't a boy any longer – but a young, smart-looking man. At his side was Cubert son of Dere – the man who'd taken his wife's clothes and yet hadn't left her so much as a note to say where he was going. He remembered their miserable skeleton smiles staring back at him from greying photos. Both had put on weight. Both were beaming. They grabbed hold of his arms and pulled him to a stand-ing position. His legs felt like rubber.

'Don't worry about the weakness,' said the man whom he now realised was Ysbaddaden, the one and only. 'It's only temporary. It's just that parts of you are still asleep. Told you those birds were good. You see, even if every single shopper in that supermarket had woken up – they still wouldn't have been able to do anything to stop us. Because the kind of sleep they drive into you, it takes the body a long time to shake it off. But most people don't even notice they've been asleep. You certainly didn't, that day at the supermarket.'

Cilydd was carried down a narrow, white corridor. Ysbaddaden disappeared down a staircase, beckoning them to follow. Cilydd's feet were hoisted up silently by the two guards, and he lay back in their arms feeling like an invalid. He tried to speak to them but they were positively mute, serene like monks, wearing pacific smiles as they looked down at him. Once they got to the bottom of the stairwell he saw another long strip ahead of them – longer, whiter, dotted with several black doors, like a hotel corridor. Outside one of these doors, Ysbaddaden came to an abrupt halt.

'This is one of our best corridors. Reserved for those that are – shall we say – *well connected*. Special clients of the organisation. Goleuddydd had a room here. And I think someone else here could shed a light on some things for you.'

He slid a metal card into a slot by the side of the door. The door opened.

'No need to knock, you see,' he said. 'He's expecting you.'

As Graid and Cubert ever so gently released him from their grasp, he heard a voice telling him to enter. He stumbled forward, grabbing on to the walls as he went, feeling the energy slowly drifting back into his legs. His first thought was how meticulous and pristine everything seemed. A little black desk. A white lamp in the corner. A silver sheen on the corner of every surface. Everything tucked away. No clutter. There was no colour anywhere. But there was life in the room. A man hunched at the far end of it, turned his head.

'Doged,' he gasped.

'Hello Cilydd,' Doged said. 'I know this must be a shock.'

Cilydd looked away. It was Gwelw who came to

his mind at that moment. Pragmatic, stoic Gwelw, who had dealt with the loss of this man in her own, quiet way. Cilydd felt the anger surfacing, and before he knew it he was lunging at Doged with all the fury he could muster. But he had misjudged the distance between them, and it left him clutching the edges of Doged's jacket rather pathetically, with Doged holding him around his waist to support him.

'Get off me!' Cilydd shouted. 'Just get away from me! How could you do this? To Gwelw? To your wife? Leave her like that! And let me take the blame for everything... I could have gone to prison for killing you!'

'It never would have happened, Cilydd, I assure you. We have ways of making sure those things don't happen... listen, I can explain it all. Just hear me out.'

Cilydd felt sick. Goleuddydd had meant to leave him. Doged had no intention of killing himself. He was in a house full of people who wanted to abandon their loved ones and play games with their emotions.

'I don't want to hear it. I want to get out of here. Back to my wife – your wife!'

He grappled to try to find a door handle. It seemed there wasn't one. He banged on the cold, white door. Nothing. Doged had taken a seat, now, as though he were warming himself up for the telling of a tale no one wanted to hear.

'Cilydd, you have to calm down. I urge you, sit here with me. There's no point in banging – they won't open the door. They decide when we get to come out, not us. That's the way of things. It's a way of keeping everyone in order, you see. What we agree to is a controlled freedom. I mean, when you think about it, freedom can be a little overrated. Too much freedom and you can get yourself into a lot of trouble, believe you me. It's not quite the same as being locked up in some cell somewhere. I mean, I've got everything I could possibly want in this room. When the door opens, I go out. If it doesn't open, I stay here. It's as simple as that. So please, Cilydd – step away from the door.'

'Are you... are you going to come back, is that it? You're ready to take my place...'

He thought of the portrait in the hallway, the one

Arthur had painted. How absurd it would all seem if Doged walked in through that front door again.

'I had no intention of ruining things for you, I promise. Gwelw and Lleuwen, the life I left behind – the one you inhabited, it's yours. At least it was. I would never take it away from you. You've done a marvellous job. Caring for them the way you did. I was sceptical at first of course, I never thought it was going to work – I never thought it would turn out the way it did. But you seemed to fit the bill better than I ever could.'

'But how do you... how do you know? I mean, have you been watching us?'

'No, of course not. But we get reports. It's all part of the deal. Except in my case, you and Gwelw... well it was Ysbaddaden's idea. There was no question about it, I had to disappear. I'd made a real mess of things at the Assembly. All those hospitals I'd shut down, all those medical botches I'd had to cover up – things were going to unravel very soon and they would take my family down with them. Night after night Gwelw would come into my study and see me hunched, crying, tearing myself to pieces over the stress of it all. You know too well what she's like – no-nonsense, seeing every problem like a bone which just needs slotting back into place, a reduction as she calls it – she just couldn't understand how much I wanted to leave it all behind. She warned me – don't do anything silly, or I will never forgive you. But I had to. As much as I loved my wife and daughter I simply had to. But in leaving them, the best I could do was make sure that they would be looked after. That's where you came in. I had to make sure someone would care about what happened to them. That's when Ysbaddaden thought of it. I know it might seem as if nothing can touch that man, but I rather think he felt quite bad about the way things turned out with your wife. That's when he came up with this – a solution – a simple act of kindness. And when he showed me your file I remembered meeting you, at the Assembly, that day. I remembered liking you. You weren't like those others – you seemed to wear your losses better somehow. I mean, I couldn't have just anyone filling my role. You seemed to be, well, determined, I suppose. A survivor. I knew she would like that about you. Not a quitter, like me.'

'But I was about to kill myself...' Cilydd said, wishing, at that particular moment, he'd succeeded.

'No, you were never going to do that. You had suicidal thoughts, of course, those were your own – but think about it – you weren't really going to do it, were you? Not until we put you right out there, on the far edge of that ledge. When you found yourself there you thought that the end had come, naturally enough. You thought there was nothing else for it but to jump. But then I came along. And you saw what a horrible thing it was – something you didn't want after all – am I right? The tumble in itself didn't actually happen like you think it did – what you witnessed as one continuous movement would not in fact have been that at all. In fact, it took us hours to manoeuvre the whole thing. I was freezing by the end of it, seemed like I'd been in that water for ages.'

Doged shivered with the memory of it. Cilydd

saw the whole thing again himself, the black, dark birds coming at him on the cliff. Turning his head. Making him sleepy, making him think there was nothing for it but to jump. And then of course there had been Doged's wilful, helping hand. The hand that was offering him a new life.

'But Gwelw, and Lleuwen. I mean... I love them. I truly, truly love them both. You couldn't have... you couldn't have organised that... you just couldn't have...' As if it had just happened he saw his hand sliding between Gwelw's legs in the community-hall car park. The passion he had felt at that moment. Was that unreal too? Was it those birds? He tried to recall if there had been any dark shadows twittering above him.

'The love, no. The passion, certainly not. That was genuine – a stroke of luck. I mean, the marriage, we anticipated. With my death on your conscience, and her turning up at the Missing Persons' Network – it was bound to drive you together. But the love you talk of now – I mean, I didn't realise you felt like that. It's... well, it's even more of a comfort I suppose. Or at least it was. Until you turned up here. I mean, I don't know what will happen now. To Gwelw and Lleuwen. I'm sure Ysbaddaden will have someone lined up for them, so I shouldn't worry about it too much.'

'What do you mean, lined up for them? As soon as I get out of here I'm...'

'Oh, Cilydd.' Doged lowered his eyes and seemed genuinely to sympathise with him. 'There's no getting out of here, once you're in. I thought you'd have understood that much. I think that's the mistake your wife made.'

'What happened to my wife?' Cilydd asked quietly. 'They never told me what happened to her.'

'From what I gather she completely changed her mind once she was here, and demanded to be let out. Of course no one lets you go once you're here. But she convinced one of the doctors who was looking after her to let her go and before anyone knew it she was halfway through the forest. That's when they set Ysbaddaden's wild boar on her, poor thing. I mean, you can only imagine how frightened she would have been. But it's the only way if someone makes a dash for it like that. Ysbaddaden never meant to kill her. I think he was hoping that the boar would just scare her, hunt her down, keep her cornered in that pigsty until someone came to retrieve her. He did everything he could to make sure she was brought back safe and well, rushing both those doctors to the site. But they were too late. It's amazing the boy survived, to be honest. And although I doubt they could have done much to save her, he was still furious with those doctors, I tell you. I've never seen him so angry. You can see why – I mean, no one had died on his watch before. The operation isn't about killing people off. It's about saving them, providing them with a haven. So those doctors had really damaged his reputation. Not that they had meant to, of course. I remember them – quite lovely people. Quite brilliant too. A man and a woman. They both used to have a room on this floor. I gather both wanted to disappear because of some medical scandal or other. Always blame the doctors, don't they? But they couldn't stay here. Not after that. He had to get rid of them.'

'Did he... did he kill them?'

'No, no, nothing like that. I gather he sent them away to the farm to run things there. I think... I think perhaps the boy went with them.'

So that's who Cilydd's parents were. Not even a couple, just two people driven together by a terrible mistake.

'I can't believe they just left her there, though... it's just so... so barbaric.'

'Well, she was dead. This isn't a house for the dead.'

'Isn't it? Aren't you all pretending to be dead?' Cilydd asked. He was angry now. Those doctors, Culhwch's makeshift parents, had left his beautiful Goleuddydd lying on her back in that pigsty. Wrenched her open like an animal. But they'd done it to save his son. He saw now the logic in Goleuddydd's command: don't remarry. She had known, in running away, what these people were capable of. What they knew about her, of him; possibly she guessed how they would interfere in his life. How they would try to fix things, and only make things worse. Like leaving her bleeding in an empty pigsty.

'We can't control what those left behind will think of us, they write their own little narratives, they believe what's best, what's easiest for them to believe. Some will keep the fire alive. Others won't. A rational, sensible woman like Gwelw will accept the facts, and won't rely on flimsy conjecture to keep her going. That's the kind of woman she is. She buried me in her mind the day they found my wax jacket, I know that much. So I'm not pretending to be dead. It's just that my absence is open to inter-pretation. And certainly here I don't feel dead, either. I may not have the freedom I once had, but what I've got is a new life. It's a quieter one. But it's a new start. Without all the usual drudgery or responsibility that life brings. Without the risk. Without the hurt. It's a perfect life in many ways.'

But your voice is dull and lifeless, Cilydd wanted to tell him. A life where you care for nothing, risk nothing, is exactly that – nothing.

Doged let out a heavy sigh and turned his head.

'I think you should go now,' he said. 'I get very tired these days when I have to talk for long periods of time. I honestly don't know how I managed it all that time in the Assembly. I'm just not used to it now. I fear it's too much for me. I'm sure they'll come for you soon.'

As soon as he'd finished the sentence the door opened and Ysbaddaden and his guards re-entered.

'I hope you enjoyed your little tête-à-tête, gentlemen. You're looking a little more enlightened now, Cilydd, less in the dark, shall we say. Thank you Doged, for saving me the trouble of explaining all that – such things really can get a little complicated, and one often forgets the exact sequence of events. Now, I think it's time we got you settled in, don't you? I think you're going to like it here, Cilydd.'

'But my boy... and Arthur,' he protested as he was dragged – ever so politely it seemed by the mute, smiling boys – out of the room.

'Oh don't worry Cilydd. The boy can come too. In fact, you can both consider yourselves officially missing. As for Arthur, well – Arthur is – and always has been – a little bit of a nuisance as far as we're concerned.'

Cilydd was staring down another spiral of stairs. They were unlike the others he'd trodden before – they were rusty and creaked as he descended. He was being dragged further and further into the heart of the building. The surroundings became more and more stark, until they were travelling in shadow, damp filling his nostrils.

'My son,' Cilydd said. 'You've got my son. What have you done with him?'

'Oh, he's fine. But he won't be running off with my daughter, I've made sure of that. You see, Olwen can't ever leave this place. Not while I'm still in the land of the living. The trouble is she knows everything. She's always known it. It's what she's grown up with, people coming, people going – she was born into it. I always wanted a child, you see. I suppose I was rather hoping that Culhwch might become mine, one day – but after what happened with Goleuddydd... well, I couldn't do it. You see, he was a horrid reminder of what happened and I had to send him away. But I wanted to make up for it. Never take on another pregnant woman – that's what my advisors told me. But I wanted to prove to them I could do it. That's just the kind of man I am. I mean, when I solved my first mystery it was like a light had descended on me. It was like I was gifted, special. And I couldn't bear never doing it again. I suppose that's why I wanted to gather up all those mysteries, solve them for myself. Be part of something. And it was the same when I found Olwen's mother. She wasn't like Goleuddydd, you understand. She was a timid little thing, just a child herself. Fourteen. Terrified of someone finding out about the pregnancy. So I took her in. She didn't have to pay, not like the others. Just give me the child, I said to her. I'll take care of it. All that time I was thinking of Culhwch, what a mess I'd made of things. Olwen was my way to put things right, you see. A lovely, natural birth it was. Her mother was so very brave. Not that Olwen has ever known that her mother is living here. She thinks it's just her and me – that was the arrangement. And you know there's something so very special about Olwen. The day she was born the fields around this place just lit up with white flowers. The purest, whitest flowers. It was like the ground forgiving me for what I'd done to poor old Culhwch. Such an unfortunate name – Culhwch – I know. But how can any of us really escape the circumstances of our birth? It's always there, you see. It was the one name we could give him. He carried the darkness of that pigsty within him – and here was Olwen, brimming with light, her name a white trail of flowers. They're so different. And I'm afraid, for that reason, they simply can't be together. This house, the house of the missing – it's her home. In some ways, she's always been missing – we never registered her birth, so technically, she doesn't even exist. And it was my hope that one day, Olwen would grow up and be part of all this. But your children, however condi-tioned they are, never turn out exactly how you planned, do they? When she fell pregnant – well you can imagine, it caused something of a stir in here. 'Who was it?' I asked her. Turns out it was Ffercos son of Poch who'd forced himself on her. A grubby little thing. You can imagine how wounded I felt.

I'm afraid I rather... I rather lost it. I suppose he was our first... deliberate fatality.'

'The word you're looking for is murder,' Cilydd said.

'Another vulgar term that is bandied about all too readily by journalists,' Ysbaddaden replied. 'I suppose Culhwch fancies himself as some sort of father to this child now, but honestly, Cilydd, how can he be? He's been living in seclusion all his life. All he's ever known is birds and make-believe. He's just a little boy.'

'That's because of you. Because you stuck him on that farm with two people who didn't even want to be his parents...'

'Not at first, no. But I gather they both developed quite a lot of affection for the boy in the end. There were times, when we took our days out to visit them, that I glimpsed real happiness in them. Contentment even. They were happy with their farm, with their little family life – even if there was no love between them. Surgeons they were, both of them. I never anticipated they'd make me the offer they did. To give me all their money so I could buy this place in my own name, and hide them there. An odd proposition, I know, but when you're a man without responsibilities and someone offers you this enormous estate – well, you're hardly going to say no, are you? And one night when we were all settled, they got the idea that I could keep tracking people down, and offer them a safe haven. For free, at first. And time after time I was surprised by how much people wanted what I was offering. Not surprising though really. When I found most of them they were holed up in bedsits and hostels, sleeping rough. And there I was, offering them a room of one's own, away from it all. Safety. But then sure enough it started getting more and more costly and we realised that we had to make people pay to come here. They had to organise it. A little tricky, isn't it, advertising something you don't want anyone to know about? But we managed it. Friends in high places, that sort of thing. It's amazing actually how many people do know we exist, but keep it firmly under their hats. Take the police, for example. Turn a blind eye to every single case thanks to our connections with the force. I mean, how else do you think we were able to move a family into the farm, even as the investigation continued? Culhwch was moved in, right under their noses. And the business slowly started coming in. As long as we kept an eye out for suitable cases, we never struggled to fill the rooms.'

'So you just picked Goleuddydd out at random?'

'Hardly. Goleuddydd was more or less volunteered to us. I mean, she comes from a very powerful family.'

Cilydd's stomach churned as the truth dawned on him at last.

'Oh my God,' he said. 'Anlawdd. Anlawdd set her up.'

'He just subtly informed her of our existence, that's all. He gave her the option, he never forced her...'

'He killed her!' Cilydd realised he was shouting now, his voice deflating as the corridor around him seemed to narrow to a thin strip. 'By sending her here he killed her, he must have known that. But then... it doesn't make sense... he was the one begging me to get Arthur on to it...'

'Yes. Indeed. Arthur. Think about it. Arthur who'd been pottering around the streets selling hand-carved animals for half his life. Arthur the street artist. Arthur the carver. Arthur, who hadn't solved a single case in his life. Get good old Arthur on to it, Cilydd. Look, I know it's a shock. But Anlawdd isn't a bad man. It just... just didn't work out as he planned, that's all. We offered the boy to Anlawdd, to make up for things, but he didn't want him. It was too painful for him, as you can imagine. But he did stress in no uncertain terms that were we to give the boy to you, he would cut our funding...'

'Funding?' His voice was no more than a pathetic whisper in the dark now. 'Anlawdd... he funds you?'

'He's not our only benefactor. There are others. Doged, for example. Like I said, you've got to have friends in high places to make an operation like this work.'

By now they had reached what looked like the dungeon of the building. A cast-iron door was wrenched open, and he was shoved hastily through it. When he turned his back he realised that this was where the journey ended, that he was being shoved into a cell. He turned around to face Ysbaddaden, as the guards walked away.

'You can't leave me here,' Cilydd protested. 'I won't be part of this! I need to be with my son.'

'I'm afraid that's not possible, Cilydd. I'm sorry, I truly am.'

The door clattered shut, and the damp settled on him like a second skin.

★

He was awoken by the chattering of birds. Fitful, fantastic bursts of song. At first he couldn't fathom where the noise was coming from, but he soon realised that it was coming from everywhere, dark wings ruffling around him in every direction. The last thing he remembered was being weak with hunger, lying on the floor, thinking he was going to die. And yet, although he still had not eaten, for what seemed like days and days, his hunger had evaporated. He felt full and energised, like he'd just had a good meal. The dark gave way to a host of piercing orange eyes, all staring up at him. He felt his way around the feathery mass, brushing against their coats as the chatter grew louder and louder. But the beaks were perfectly still between his fingers, politely shut.

Something rattled. Suddenly the door that was sure never to be open to him again, was pulled back, and light flooded in. In front of him was Culhwch. His eyes, Goleuddydd's pale green eyes, were strong and determined.

'Culhwch,' he said, feeling once again the urge to throw his arms around his son, to pull his flesh and blood towards him. 'It's good to see you. I'm so glad you're... you're OK,' he added, resting an arm tentatively on his shoulder. 'I thought for a moment they might have... well, you know...'

'I'm absolutely fine,' his son replied. 'They tried to lock me up but I'm fine. But we've got a chance now, a chance to get out of here. And we have to do it quickly.'

Birds hovered in the air between them, a rush of feathers in their faces.

'What on earth are these birds doing? How did they get in here?'

'I think Olwen must have released them through the air vents,' Culhwch said. 'She told me to wait for a sign. The birds... well they seem to me like a sign. I don't know how they did it but they seem to have unlocked my cell. When I woke up I felt, well, like I've never felt before. Do you feel it too? A lightness. Yes, that's it, much lighter than before. Like I've never eaten anything in my life, and will never need to again. I feel I could do anything. We can leave now, can't we. We'll get Olwen and we'll leave.'

'But Ysbaddaden, and the guards...' Cilydd said, hating to dent his son's bravado but finding himself adopting a grave tone, preparing his son for the worst. Wasn't that what real parents found themselves doing, time after time? Bursting their children's bubbles? He had never had to do it with Lleuwen. Gwelw did the disciplining, and then he cajoled her with hot chocolate and wan smiles in the aftermath. But now he felt it – an urge to be firm, to tell it like it was.

'We're not going to get out. Not with those guards around the place. Or the security. I think we have to face facts here Culhwch.'

Culhwch shook his head, a laugh brimming across his lips.

'No, you don't understand. It will be easy. Look. Just look.'

Cilydd followed his son out into the corridor. Right next to the door were Graid and Cubert. Slumped against the wall, curling into one another – a pair of sinking question marks. Eyes firmly shut. Emanating tiny, peaceful exhalations. He turned back to look at his son.

'Everyone else in this building is asleep, Cilydd, everyone – the guards outside my cell were too, the guards at the top of the stairs – everybody. Everybody's asleep but us. It's Olwen's sign – she's calling us, giving us an opportunity to save her... we have to get her and leave. I promised her, remember?'

'But why... I mean do you really think it's wise to go and get her? If we can get out, I think we should just get out,' Cilydd said, seeing, with sudden clarity, that Olwen was a mere nuisance. He had never wanted Olwen. He only wanted his son.

'Olwen is the reason we came. And more than that – if you ask me – Olwen's the reason we're still alive. Ysbaddaden would gladly let us rot down here. Just trust me. You're... you're my father. I need you to support me in this.'

Father. The word jolted him, sending electrical impulses all around his body. It wasn't wholly unfamiliar – for Lleuwen sometimes called him *Father*, sardonically, wrinkling her nose at him – even Dad – but every time he heard it, he felt a pang of guilt, and could not help but think of her real *father* – Doged, tumbling over the rocks. Now it was a free word. Free as a bird. And so he did what he thought a proper father should do and followed his son back down a dark corridor, back towards chaos and disaster. The birds followed them.

'So you've seen Olwen?' he whispered into the back of his son's head.

'Yes,' he whispered back. 'Once you and Arthur fell asleep that trail sprang up again. I was becoming sleepy too and I knew if I didn't follow it right there and then it would all be over. Wherever the flowers were it seemed doors would open, gates would open for me, just like that. I just kept following those flowers until I was inside – and Olwen was waiting for me. She looked terrified. And so tired. 'I can't have the baby here,' she kept on saying. So I tried to carry her. But we didn't make it very far. Ysbaddaden and the guards, they were right behind us the whole time – teasing us, letting us think we could escape and then seizing us right at the last minute. Then he... I don't know. He took Olwen. Just before he took her she told me: 'It's not over. The birds will help us. Wait for the birds. They'll know what to do.' Ysbaddaden seemed – well, not what I was expecting, really. Even as we were walking down here he was trying to assure me I was going to be reunited with you. But then he left me in that cell. Left me there to die.'

'But what happened to Arthur?'

'I don't know where Arthur went,' he said. 'I haven't seen him since the forest.'

Cilydd tried to remember what Ysbaddaden had said about Arthur. Meddling Arthur would be punished, he had said. He shoved the thought to the back of his mind as they travelled further into the building. The quiet that surrounded them was not peaceful, somehow, but tinged with foreboding. He recalled something that Ysbaddaden had said about the birds. About them waking the dead. Was he dead? Was that it? The birds filled every corner with their feathers and noise. They came upon a large hall – chandeliers dangled from the high ceilings, white corridors splayed out in every direction, and portraits of the residents adorned the walls. Underneath each one was a note about their disappearance. As he rushed past he felt as though they were laughing at him, these great big oil incarnations of those tiny little photographs he'd held in the palm of his grieving hand, so many years ago. They paused suddenly in front of a face they both recognised.

'Doged,' said Culhwch. 'Isn't it? Your wife's so-called dead husband?'

'Yes,' he said. 'You know, I never killed him. He's

here. Alive and well. Did your parents tell you about Doged? Was that it? Did they tell you I killed him?'

'I found it in Arthur's notes. The day I arrived in the town I broke into Arthur's flat. I was searching for things – anything I could find. I saw it scribbled in Arthur's notes. 'I think Cilydd has something to do with Doged's death.' It was such a little detail – he may not really have even believed it at the time. But it was all I had. And when I heard your voice all shaky on the phone I thought, well, I thought it must be true.'

This left Cilydd reeling. The thought that Arthur had begun to investigate him – to suspect him. And yet he saw that Arthur had more intuition than he gave him credit for. Arthur, for all his vagueness and indecision, had read something in him after all.

Culhwch finally hesitated by a door at the far end of the building. The birds twittered and screeched around them, rupturing the silence. They flocked to the door, covering every inch of it, a brawny dark force, until the door gave way. The birds swept in, gathering in a little coven around a bed by the window. When their feathers had stilled, he saw a blonde-haired girl lying there, with a ballooning stomach. Right next to her, slumped unconscious in his chair, was Ysbaddaden Bencawr. Culhwch knelt by the bed and stroked his lover's hair.

'I've come to get you...' Culhwch said. 'Me and my father, we'll get you out of here. If we go now we'll be away before everyone wakes up.'

The birds were getting frantic, poking around in the room, pecking ferociously at things. One of them got hold of a pillow and started to wave it around like a flag. Another joined it, tugging and tugging at the seams until eventually the cotton ripped, sending a splay of feathers over the bed. These feathers were pale and long, at odds with their own dark wings – duck feathers, or goose. Many others descended and collected them in their beaks, laying them down on the ground to form a trail. The biggest bird in the room shook a gust of them over Ysbaddaden's head. 'What are they doing?' Cilydd asked Olwen. Her beauty took him off guard, and he saw what his son saw – something quite extraordinary, a porcelain perfection – fragile, breakable – he wanted to cup her in his hand. Hold up her up to the light. Her eyes seemed almost transparent, looking not at him, but through him, somehow. She held out her fingers to the birds and they shuffled towards her.

'They're faithful creatures. My father has always prided himself on it. But what he doesn't know is how easily they change allegiances. For years now, they've been on my side. They're Rhiannon's birds after all, they're conditioned to respond better to women. Or to those on the margins. Lonely people, yes, they like their lonely people. They'll follow a lonely soul to the ends of the earth, all the while singing a sweet melody, trying to comfort them. They've comforted me for years, you see. Ysbaddaden lost his power over them a long time ago – though he's never realised it. Because they keep up the charade. But anyone who looks closely enough knows what they're doing. And what they're doing now is imitating me. They create their own white trail wherever they go, from whatever they can find.'

It slowly dawned on Cilydd. The flour aisle. The

white shells on the ledge after Doged's fall. All the while Ysbaddaden believed that the birds were working for him while they were merely executing their silent rebellion, waiting to undo him.

'I'm so happy you came Culhwch,' Olwen said, stroking his hand. 'I really am. I feel that, I feel that I could truly love you. But I can't come with you. I'm too... too heavy. And the baby's near. So near now. I can't ask you to carry this burden with me.'

'It's not a burden... we'll sort it out. My father... my father has a house. We can bring up the baby together. All of us. Can't we... Dad?'

Cilydd looked down at Olwen, but all he saw this time was Goleuddydd. Making a run for it in the forest. Giving in to the darkness and the damp in that pigsty. He had a bad feeling about that baby. He didn't want it in his house. It was nothing to do with him. But he nodded his head silently, all the same.

'It's up to Olwen,' he said. 'We can't force her to come if she doesn't want to. What do you want, Olwen?'

There was a muted anger in his voice, and he

realised he was not speaking to Olwen at all but to Goleuddydd. What had she wanted, all those years ago? What on earth had driven her here, of all places? He was angry. Angry at her for being such a wilful, silly wife – thinking she was so eccentric, making wild, inappropriate choices because it seemed like fun. Because it seemed like *living*. All he wanted now was to be reunited with Gwelw. Lovely, sensible Gwelw, whose business was fixing other people, making sure something as essential, as important, as their bones were in order – who would click things back into place in one swift movement, with a smile.

Olwen rose to her feet uncertainly and walked towards her father. The birds moved with her as she got closer to him, scattering more of the spindly goose down across his body.

'You're right, Culhwch, I can't stay any longer. The baby... the baby needs to be safe. If we wait too long it might... it might die. And even if it doesn't, there isn't any kind of life here for a child. But it's only if Ysbaddaden dies that I can start living. He has to die. Do you understand?'

Cilydd looked at Culhwch and Culhwch looked at Cilydd.

'We can't... we can't kill him,' Cilydd said, laughing nervously. 'That makes us no better than him. And besides, we'll be... we'll be prosecuted, and I'm not risking that...'

'No one's going to be prosecuted for anything, haven't you realised that yet? This has been going on for years and years and the police, the government, everyone – they've let it happen. They'll find some way of bringing it all to a halt if he dies. No one's going to look into it, trust me. It needs to stop. It can only stop if Ysbaddaden dies. Otherwise, I'm staying here.'

She sat back down on the bed, her cold eyes challenging them both. Ysbaddaden's eyes flickered momentarily, but he remained solidly asleep. Neither Cilydd nor Culhwch uttered a word.

'OK, well, I'll shave him, then,' said Olwen suddenly, pushing herself back up. 'He needs a good shave – he's simply not had the time these last couple of days, what with all the excitement that's been going on around here. Yes, a good shave. Clean him up, good and proper.'

For a moment Cilydd thought that the dark thought had passed suddenly and that Olwen was stepping back from the murderous brink of her thoughts. But then he saw her hands trembling as she assembled the equipment. She swished some lather in a bowl and rinsed a razor under the tap.

'Yes, that's right,' she muttered to herself. 'I'll start off by lathering him up, and then perhaps one of you two could... could finish things.'

Olwen's hands worked quickly over Ysbaddaden's face, moving in swift, white circles, foaming tiny waves all over his face. The more she gushed the sicker Cilydd felt. He was up on that ledge again, watching Doged fall. Except this time, he really was going to push someone. Slit someone open like someone had slit his own wife open. Ysbaddaden's head tilted back, and the pale white throat seemed to grin at him.

He saw Culhwch step forward. He pulled him back.

'I think you two should go now,' he said, in a voice

he did not recognise as his own. 'I think you should start moving before people start waking up.' He gave Olwen a meaningful nod as he took the razor away from her. 'I'll take over here.'

The steel was against his hand – cold and urgent.

Olwen nodded appreciatively at him and got up to leave the room. Culhwch helped her to the door. Neither one of them looked back. He listened to their footsteps receding down the corridor. The birds, in a confused flurry, flitted back and forth across the room as if not knowing whether they should stay or go. A few remained, hanging on the huge, cast-iron curtain rails, with one bird swinging upside down, its huge orange claws grappling with the dull gold. Cilydd stared down at Ysbaddaden's face, and rested the razor on his neck.

Was it really just a matter of sliding it against the skin? And then how would he know where to stop? The blade glinted at him, dazzling him. It didn't look sharp enough. If it wasn't sharp enough, it might get stuck. He might only cut enough to wake Ysbaddaden up. Maybe he should try it out first on himself. He looked down at his own body. What bits of himself could he try to cut? He raised a finger up to the light. Just a little prick, just to see how sharp it was. Then he saw how ridiculous it was, this dilly-dallying, turning the knife on himself. Thinking that he had to suffer first, if he was going to hurt someone else. If you're going to do it, just do it. He was reminded of Gwelw at that moment, how she hated his indecision, his tendency to circumnavigate. Often, when they were going out to some event, some party or other, he'd make things complicated. Suggest going somewhere for a drink first, or to call in at a friend's house. Gwelw would just do up her seatbelt and say quite firmly: 'If I'm going to a party, then *I'm going to a party*,' and he'd drive straight there, forgetting all the other engagements, which he could see, on arrival, were just not necessary.

He stared back down at Ysbaddaden's neck. This was it. He was going to the party.

And just as he was about to do it, one of the birds twitched, and the door creaked open. He looked up. Standing in the doorframe was Arthur. He'd been severely beaten, his cheeks grazed and purple. One arm was held awkwardly at an angle, as though it were broken.

'If you don't mind, I'd like to do the honours,' he said, limping forward. He was barefoot – even his toes were bleeding. A few of the birds, who'd been perfectly still until then, began to twitter. Their orange eyes slid towards Arthur. Then, it seemed, one by one, they flocked to him. Perching themselves on his shoulders, his back. One stood boldly on his head. 'Arthur,' he said, walking towards his cousin. 'What happened to you?'

'Oh, nothing a warm bath won't heal,' he smiled wanly. 'I suppose it's only what I deserve for meddling so much these past years. Told you these cases had a connection, didn't I?'

Arthur limped over to the chair where Ysbaddaden was sleeping. The tyrant's throat rose and fell in fleshy gurgles, he rolled and winced, but still he did not wake up. How small people looked when they were sleeping, Cilydd thought, even the most powerful ones. They had no choice but to abandon every sense of themselves and become primal, thrashing, open-mouthed things. The birds looked quizzically down at their former master. One of them swooped down and tugged at an eyebrow. Plucking it right out, it drew blood, and a small kernel of life bubbled to the surface. It was evident that he had lost any power he had over them, for these birds seemed ready to destroy him now.

Arthur straightened himself. The birds stood to attention. They were waiting for Arthur's lead.

'He looks just like I remember him,' Arthur said. 'Smug, self-serving. Thinking he's got it all. He was like that even before all this happened.'

Arthur fished around in the top pocket of Ysbaddaden's suit and retrieved a silver card. Cilydd recognised this as the very same silver card that had allowed him access to Doged's room. Arthur held it up, letting the light bounce back and forth on its surface.

'It's bizarre, isn't it – how a locked room can become a haven? I mean, people say it all the time, don't they. Lock me up and throw away the key. No doubt we've all thought it at times, that it would be nice to disappear, to have someone else take responsibility for us, keep us away from everything? It's just I can't believe they were all so compliant. So quiet. Sitting in their little rooms, only being allowed out when he slid the magic card in the slot. It's odd isn't it? It's like those birds send everyone into a trance or something.'

Cilydd didn't think anything was odd anymore. Goleuddydd, Anlawdd, Doged — they'd all locked him into a room and thrown away the key a long time ago. They'd made him a prisoner in his own life. 'I can guarantee you,' continued Arthur, 'that even if I opened every single door on every corridor, opened those doors wide, they still wouldn't leave. But if we... if we somehow got them all outside — out of this house, into the fresh air — most of them would snap out of it. The question is how do you convince them to leave? Even with Ysbaddaden dead, they're still going to want to stay. Which reminds me, I think you should give me the razor now, Cilydd. It really doesn't suit you.'

Cilydd had not realised how tightly he was gripping the blade until Arthur tried to prize it away from him.

'Oh really? It doesn't suit me? Like Doged's death didn't suit me? Come on Arthur, I know you suspected me. For all I know you still do.'

'Look, Cilydd. When you're a private investigator you suspect everybody. You don't just go for the obvious choices. All I know is that when I gave you that picture on your wedding day, you were unsettled. There was something about it you didn't like. And it was the fact that it was yourself, and not Doged, that was in that picture. I could read the guilt all over you. But really, now. It's OK. I don't care what happened. I don't even care if you killed him...'

'I didn't kill him! Let go of my arm...'

They struggled in silence until the razor suddenly fell and clattered against the marble flooring. Ysbaddaden thrashed again, eyeballs turning like small tides beneath his eyelids.

'Cilydd,' Arthur said firmly, grabbing him by the shoulders. 'Your son is waiting for you by the front door. He's trying to get Olwen out only... only she won't move. She knows, Cilydd. She knows you haven't done it. It's like that doorstep is some kind of boundary and she won't be able to cross it unless he's dead. If we don't kill him, we'll never get out of here, I promise you. And you're not going to do it, are you? I think you should leave it to me.'

'But what... I mean, what happens then? After he dies? I mean all these people... and his body, and...'

Arthur looked away from him.

'I'll sort it. It'll be fine. I'll make sure they all get out. I'll find a way. Just take care of yourself Cilydd. And the boy. Be happy. Let yourself be happy now. It'll be fine. Everything will be fine.'

He knew from Arthur's voice that it would not be fine.

The front door was wide open, brimming with birds. On seeing him they all started to fly upwards towards Olwen's bedroom, as though they, too, were keen to see what Arthur would do. The forest outside somehow seemed smaller than the night before.

There was a chill in the air, the fir trees sheathed in a frosty fog. Olwen leaned against the doorframe, her eyes meeting his for the first time. Cilydd almost felt the blade, as though it were cutting through his own neck.

'Arthur!' he shouted, panic seizing him. 'Arthur!'

There was no noise at all. No sign of Arthur. The house seemed completely still. Even the chattering of birds seemed to have stopped.

Olwen clutched a single feather in her hand. She rolled it back between thumb and forefinger.

'So the birds have a new owner,' she said, smiling. Her fingers trailed around the doorframe. She shut her eyes. 'It won't be long now before everything changes. Before it all comes crashing down.'

'Please Olwen...' said Culhwch, trying to coax his pregnant lover through the door. 'Look, I think it's best we go now. You can come back here. We'll bring you back, after all this is over.'

She laughed.

'There's no going back Culhwch. He's dead. If he's dead, and I leave, then this house – this house will fall, don't you understand? It's my presence here that's been keeping the place on its feet. I've given it life, new hope. That's why he had to have a child here. Only a child's presence could give the place hope. Nothing to do with him wanting to be a father. You were his first hope, of course, but like you know, that didn't work out. You had too much darkness inside you. Children are feral beings. They know the circumstances of their own birth even if they don't have the means to express it. He had to get rid of the ill feeling from the house, it was too potent, too destructive. Then I came – a second chance. And for so many years I knew nothing of pain, of separation, loneliness. This was just the way of things. Until things happened. Until I started to lose belief. And then they needed another child... that's when they sent Ffercos son of Poch to me. Poor old Ffercos.' She went quiet, as though sparing a thought for him. 'You could see in his eyes he hated every second of it as much as I did. Every time he was sent to me, you'd see that reluctance in him, it took him ages to... well, you know. Poor, poor Ffercos.'

Olwen finally stepped out into the light. Culhwch took her hand to steady her.

'Don't be too hard on those parents of yours, Culhwch, your guardians, whatever you want to call them. Your mother, you know, she was very kind to me when I was at the farm. She was such a gentle woman, really. Ysbaddaden couldn't have taken too kindly to her letting you go like that. From what I hear the farm's been packed up and deserted now. It's like they were never there. It's because of me, Culhwch, that you can never go back, you do understand that? You can never go back. Neither one of us can.'

She leaned into him and kissed him gently on the mouth.

'I don't want to go back,' Culhwch said. 'I want to go forward. With you and my family. I need to get back on track, follow the path I should have been on in the first place. My father will make sure we both get back on that track, won't you Cilydd?'

All Cilydd knew at that moment was that he felt increasingly uneasy under the shadow of the great

house. Something told him that whatever the undoing of the operation would be, it was already at
work behind those towering walls. He wanted to
leave, right now, before the past toppled on them and
buried them forever. He slung Olwen's right arm
over his shoulder and motioned to his son to take
her left. They trudged slowly back through the
forest. Neither one of them looked back. Cilydd
wondered whether it really was falling behind them,
brick by brick, the foundations crumbling to dust.
What would become of all those who lived there?
Would they, as Olwen put it, 'fall' too? When they
got to the road, they helped Olwen into the car. She
stared at it as though it was a wondrous creation, her
fingers leaving dirty smudges on the windowpane.
Cilydd climbed into the driver's seat.

'Where now?' Cilydd said, more to himself than to
anyone else.

He caught a glimpse of Culhwch and Olwen in
his rear-view mirror. Their bodies were turned away
from each other, staring out of separate windows.
Culhwch opened the door and got out.

'I should get Arthur,' he said. 'He brought me this far. I owe him.'

'Culhwch, we really haven't got time for this and...'

'Take her home with you. Arthur and I will be with you soon.'

Before he had time to protest, his son was gone. Gone as he had feared in the forest, gone like a pregnant woman from a supermarket. Olwen's reflection smiled uncertainly at him. The only certainty he had at that moment was that Arthur's squeaking carpentry van would deliver them safely back into the town, and so he put the keys in the ignition and drove, trying not to think of anything at all, clearing a white space in his mind like the one in Arthur's flat. Cilydd watched Olwen taking it all in, the flurry of activity in the town, the peculiar noises, the huff and puff of city life – her translucent eyes darting about wildly in her head, while the dome that was her body remained entirely still. He drove and drove until he found himself back at the house. Even when he got there, he could not quite fathom that the house he saw in front of him was his home. It seemed unreal to him now; a stranger's abode, for the person he had been when he left was now absent.

Curtains flickered. He saw Gwelw's face look confusedly at him through the patio doors. She came out in her slippers.

'Where on earth have you been? I was worried about you! The way you were acting before we left I was worried you might have... might have,' she paused, suddenly noticing the figure in the back of the car. 'Is that... is that a girl? Cilydd, there's a girl in the back of your car.' Gwelw squashed her face up against the glass. He knew that she'd spotted the stomach. That big, round stomach that was like some accusing eye. 'Oh my God, Cilydd what have you been doing?'

'I've... I've...' he looked behind him. Olwen was asleep. Mouth open, head lolled back. He wished he had something to cover that exposed neck of hers. He got out of the car. Much to his surprise, the air that had been cool a few hours ago was now soupy and hot, and he felt suddenly as though his whole world were melting. In front of his eyes he saw tiny little snow-like flecks. Except he knew it couldn't be snowing, not at this time of year.

'Get inside, will you,' Gwelw said bluntly. 'And get the girl in too. Whoever she is. I'm not going to be held responsible for damaging that baby, no matter what you've done. The advice is to stay indoors.'

'What do you mean... whose advice?'

Lleuwen was standing in the doorway, watching him with a bemused look.

'Who's Dad got there?'

'Your guess is as good as mine, cariad. But right now we must deal with the task at hand and get everyone back inside.'

Olwen was ushered in without a further word. Cilydd stood in the garden looking up at the sky. By now the white flecks were coming in fast, falling on his face, irritating his eyes. When he entered the house, he found Olwen sprawled on the sofa in front of the television, bulging out of the upholstery – an elephant in the room if there ever was one. Lleuwen was not subtle in her disgust; her eyes curved all the way around Olwen's stomach, before looking back at Cilydd with a mixture of confusion and condemnation. Gwelw had her back turned to him. God knows what she must think, Cilydd thought. The way he'd been acting when she left, his nervousness, his panic. Now she'd returned to find him practically monosyllabic with a pregnant teenager on his hands, what should she think?

Lleuwen finally stopped staring at Olwen and turned back towards the screen.

'Dad, I think you better look at this... it's totally mad...'

On the twenty-four-hour news channel there was footage of a forest in flames. The blaze was ravaging the fir trees, each one alight, their tall heads softening swiftly, turning in on themselves. Next there was footage of a building, where the fire was said to have started. Cilydd froze. It was Ysbaddaden's mansion. Outside the building, there were several clusters of people, all looking shell-shocked, being helped to their feet by the emergency services. The cameras zoomed in on them. There they all were. Glittering like fish in their foil blankets – Cadwy son of Geraint, Fflewddwr Fflam Wledig, Rhuawn Bebyr son of Dorath, Bradwen son of Moren Mynog, Dalldaf son of Cimin Cof, and many, many others, thrust from obscurity back into the light of day. In their midst he saw a gaunt, albino woman who looked like an older version of Olwen. A little to her left, four fire-fighters were trying to restrain a creature of some sort. Cilydd could make out the icy glint of a fang, the grey stump of a snout, and something went through him; he had to turn away.

He wondered whether the families of the missing were watching.

What would they think, when they saw those little faces crinkling up against the light, trying to avert the camera's gaze?

Oh God, he thought, suddenly. *Doged.*

He forced himself to look again. The camera seemed to be zooming in closer and closer to the crowd. Lleuwen's eyes were glued to the screen. He saw the tip of one shiny forehead that could be Doged's, one camera shot away. He knew he was a moment away from exposure, the rest of his life hanging by a thread.

'Lleuwen, cariad. Switch it off now.'

'Don't be stupid,' she slapped his hand away from the remote. 'I want to hear more about the bodies.'

'What bodies?'

'They've recovered two bodies. They think one of them is the millionaire guy. They're not sure who the other one is. One of the partygoers.'

'Partygoers?'

'Keep up with the story, Dad.'

Partygoers. So that would be the official police line. Ysbaddaden was having a party. It may have lasted years, but it was really only just a party. No harm done.

Apart from the bodies. Two bodies. Something inside him crimped and crumbled, like the tops of the trees he saw blackening in front of him.

A pretty news reporter was now telling them that people in the surrounding area were being advised to stay indoors and place towels under their doors. The fire was fierce, and it was spreading quickly.

Firefighters were tackling the building. Cilydd stared at the television. There it was, in all its glory – the mansion, smoke billowing out of the windows, those tiny windows, one by one, cracking in the heat. White bulbous eyes exploding.

'Turn it off,' he said again.

'I know what you're doing Cilydd,' his wife whispered, pulling him aside. 'Don't think you can distract us from this. Are you going to tell me who the hell that girl is?'

'It's very hard to explain right now,' he said, keeping one eye nervously on the television screen.

'Well you have to try, Cilydd, because from the looks of her she's going to give birth any time now, and if I'm going to have to deliver a baby in my own home I at least deserve an explanation as to how that baby got there in the first place. Is it yours?'

'No, don't be ridiculous... look, just give me a moment, OK?'

The room seemed to be caving in on him. Against his wife's wishes, he removed the damp flannel by the front door, and walked out into the street.

Whiteness abounded, but it was the wrong kind of whiteness, a greying, fetid matter that poured from the sky, settling on his eyelids, penetrating his hair, making him feel dirty. Smoke snaked into his lungs. Ysbaddaden's awful stench was around him everywhere. It reminded him how close he had always been to his son – that mansion was close enough for anything that happened within it to be felt here. Its stillness and quietude had been around him all that time, suffocating him, and now so was the devastation, the destruction. But he felt further away than ever. Wherever Arthur and Culhwch were now, they were not with him. Possibly he would never see either of them again. Two bodies. It was an awful equation he was trying to work out. If they were both dead: Ysbaddaden could still be alive. But no, he had seen the certainty in Olwen's eyes when she left the house. One of them was definitely Ysbaddaden. He suddenly resented the girl on his sofa, the girl he could hear, even now, groaning and huffing as his wife, ever the doctor – even through gritted teeth – was giving her words of encouragement. Telling her she was doing really well and that she shouldn't try to fight the pain, but give in to it.

'Don't let it be Culhwch,' he said, the words escaping into the air.

He peered in through the window. Watching the TV from a distance, with the muted effect of the windowpane, was somehow easier. It gave the whole thing a feeling of unreality, of pure fiction, and yet the heat outside and the smoke – making him cough, probably doing irreparable damage to his lungs – tugged at his insides and told him it was really happening. He didn't want to be protected from the smoke. He didn't want to wait for it to pass. He wanted to breathe in the whole sorry situation.

Olwen had her head against the lounge wall; Gwelw was stroking her back. Lleuwen was glued to the television. Suddenly, like a bolt, two faces appeared on the screen – the identities of the two men that had been recovered. Ysbaddaden was there, eyes ghoulish and dark, staring back at him. But the second face threw him off guard completely. He tried to stop the rise of the awful joy within him.

The second body was Doged's.

Gwelw had not seen it yet. As ever her attention was on the task at hand; getting a baby out safely without overly staining the white carpet. Olwen was holding on to the wall; spreading her legs. Lleuwen dropped her mug of tea on the floor.

Cilydd pushed himself back from the windowsill and walked into the driveway. He walked as quickly as he could, out into the deserted street. Behind him, he heard a wail – but by now he was too far away to be able to tell which of the three women had unleashed it, and all too soon a siren had swept it away. Doged was dead. Finally dead. He thought again of Arthur's eyes as that door closed on him and Ysbaddaden. 'It'll be fine,' he'd said. Had Arthur left him there to die? Realising what it would mean to release him? Or was it the building that decided? Perhaps it was finally Doged's time to fall.

There was no traffic. No movement. Only a slight quiver of wind, dense with the flavour of fire. Exhaustion was bringing him to his knees, making him sink into the hot tarmac. He couldn't move, even when he heard footsteps approaching. Staring into the sky, in the midst of the silvery shower, he saw a face. His son.

'Culhwch,' he said. 'My boy.'

His son's face was blackened, his clothes were tattered. But the smile that broke through the ravaged flesh was white and clean.

'Yes, I'm back,' Culhwch said. 'And I'm not going anywhere from now on. Neither is anyone else. No one's going to go missing for a very long time.'

'Where's Arthur?'

'He's here, isn't he? He told me to meet him here. He left hours ago. He should be here by now. He said he was... returning the birds. Yes, he definitely said something about the birds. Don't tell me he's...'

'Missing, yes...' Cilydd said, before rolling over and putting his face to the tarmac. In his mind's eye he saw a lonely figure walking away from that burning building, making a decision not to go back, abandoning himself to the wilderness. Walking away from what he had done, Ysbaddaden's blood still fresh on his fingertips. Searching in the midst of all that chaos for that clean, white space – like the one he created in his flat all those years ago. Following his own white trail away from his own life. But he wouldn't be alone, now. Because he had the birds. The birds who were only faithful to one leader. The birds who were drawn to loneliness, to separateness. Who would help him slip away wherever – whenever – he chose.

His son's strong arms were on his shoulders, pulling him back to his feet.

'We've got to get back to Olwen,' Culhwch said. 'Come on, please. Take me to Olwen. She is alright, isn't she? Olwen? She's still with you? The baby... we need to make sure the baby's OK.'

Cilydd nodded, before turning on his heels and leading his son back towards the house. And the fug seemed at that moment to give way, illuminating a pathway of clean air for them, right back to the house. The moment he arrived outside, Cilydd knew everything had changed. Gwelw's neat lawn was awash with white flowers. He could not take his eyes off them; tens of tiny pale heads, a gathering of lost souls. He plucked at one, but it would not budge. He plucked at another – still the flower remained, rooted, unwilling to be displaced. And that's when he heard it.

Somewhere behind the door to his old life, a small cry rose up into the air. A cry which grew bolder, hungrier, with every passing moment, enticing Culhwch into the shadowy hallway. Cilydd remained outside on the doorstep, his feet unable to cross the boundary into the rest of his life.

He listened as the cry came at him again and again, bright as birdsong, piercing as grief. And yet it was neither of those things. Just a simple cry, the first attempt at being heard, at being present.

Cilydd felt something inside him buckle as its light, white notes rose up to greet the ashen rain.

How Culhwch Won Olwen
a synopsis

Cilydd, son of Celyddon, married Goleuddydd, daughter of Anlawdd Wledig. Goleuddydd became pregnant and from that moment on she went mad. When she was due to give birth her senses returned and she found herself with a swineherd and his pigs. Out of fear of the pigs she gave birth and the swineherd kept the boy until he came to court. He was baptised Culhwch, because he was found in a pig run, but he was of noble descent, a cousin to Arthur, and was placed with foster parents.

After the birth Goleuddydd became ill, but before she died she told Cilydd never to marry again until briars grew on her grave. She told her chaplain to clean the grave but after seven years he neglected this duty and Cilydd searched for a wife. One of his counsellors suggested the wife of King Doged, so they went to get her, killed the king and brought back his wife and her only daughter.

One day his new wife was told about Cilydd's son, Culhwch, and asked to see him. She wanted him to marry her daughter but he said he was not old enough. So she swore he would never get any woman apart from Olwen, daughter of Ysbaddaden Bencawr. Culhwch became full of desire for Olwen, though he knew nothing about her. His father told him to go to King Arthur and ask for Olwen as a gift.

Culhwch rode to King Arthur's court and, recognising his kinsman, Arthur agreed to his request and sent messengers to search for Olwen. After a year no one had found her, so Cai, Bedwyr and other knights set out with Culhwch on the quest. After crossing a great plain they saw a huge fort. As they came close they met a shepherd who told them the fort belonged to Ysbaddaden Bencawr. He told them to go home as no one on their quest ever left alive. But the shepherd's wife told them that Olwen came to her every Saturday to wash her hair. It was said that white clovers sprung up where she walked.

When Olwen arrived, Culhwch asked her to go with him, but she told him to ask her father. Killing his guards, the knights met with Ysbaddaden Bencawr who set Culhwch forty seemingly impossible tasks. One of these was to bring him the birds of Rhiannon, that wake the dead and lull the living to sleep. Another was to dress his stiff beard to be shaved, which could only be done by using the comb of Twrch Trwyth, a magical wild boar. Culhwch promised to fulfil the tasks, win Olwen and kill Ysbaddaden. The hunt for the Twrch Trwyth and other wonders took the knights and Arthur to Ireland and Cornwall and caused many deaths, but eventually the comb was taken from between his ears and Arthur drove him out of Cornwall into the sea.

Culhwch, Gorau son of Custennin and others took the wonders to Ysbaddaden, and Caw, son of Prydyn shaved off his beard, flesh and skin to the bone, and both his ears. Ysbaddaden agreed

HOW CULHWCH WON OLWEN

Culhwch had won, thanks to Arthur, and then Gorau cut off his head. The knights returned home, and that is how Culhwch won Olwen, daughter of Ysbaddaden Bencawr.

Synopsis by Penny Thomas
for the full story see *The Mabinogion, A New Translation*
by Sioned Davies (Oxford World's Classics, 2007).

.

Afterword

'It is easy for me to get that, though you may think it's not easy,' are Culhwch's defiant words to Ysbaddaden when he is set forty tasks to win the hand of Olwen. Ysbaddaden, not to be outdone by the young man's bravado retaliates with: 'Though you may get that, there is something you will not get,' adding complex twists to each and every task which are intended to confound his rival. As things pan out, of course, Culhwch is too clever by half – for not only does he 'get that' – he gets everything, Olwen's hand, Ysbaddaden's kingdom, and a whole lot more. But Ysbaddaden is keen to point out to his young adversary that he has – in effect – cheated in his quest, for he has employed the help of others. 'Thank Arthur,' he says, 'the man who arranged it for you.'

And he has a point – it is Arthur's right-hand man, Gorau son of Custennin, who ends up chopping off Ysbaddaden's head and brandishing it around for all to see. Culhwch, at that point, is too busy getting it on with Olwen.

This whole conversation seemed somehow symbolic of my own efforts as I went about adapting Culhwch and Olwen into a fictional novella. As adaptation is a feature of my creative work (as a bilingual author I find myself almost continuously adapting my Welsh language novels and stories into English 'versions' of their former selves), I had rather imprudently believed that this particular task was going to be easy. Or at least *easier,* by far, than adapting my own work, for I felt there would be less temptation to tamper with a work that was so thematically rich, so distinctive in its construction. I fell in love with the Mabinogion as a child, going on, in adolescence to embark on a love affair with the likes of Gwydion, Gilfaethwy, Pwyll and Lleu as I studied them for my Welsh A Levels. Even having to read it in Middle Welsh didn't put me off – it just added to the esoteric allure – here was something that was uniquely ours, yet had all the flavour of a European epic. When I received the invitation to be part of Seren's series, it felt like an old flame had come knocking – and the notion of freeing the whole thing up, of taking liberties with the text, of scribbling over the original Middle Welsh in modern English, seemed deliciously subversive, an act I'd have never been permitted in the classroom.

But I should have taken heed of Ysbaddaden's words – for there were several things that I could 'not get' when I went in search of them, and completing my quest was far from easy. The more I delved into the tale, the more I read and reread it the task ahead of me seemed overwhelming. I had forgotten how multifarious, expansive, and complex Culhwch and Olwen was; wild boars running this way and that, hags slaughtered left, right and centre, a hundred warriors or so, a ghastly step-mother, a horrible birth, a violent bloodbath, and several quests. How on earth would I rework these 'forty tasks' within a fictional framework? How would I incorporate almost a hundred of Arthur's warriors? And furthermore – how on earth was I to communicate what this story was really about – did I even know? Not to mention the vast geographic sprawl of the tale which takes the reader on heady, speedy trips to Ireland, then to Cornwall, and back over to Preseli, without pausing for breath. I found myself exhausted before I had begun; hounded by questions. What were the dark forces that drove Culhwch to chase Olwen, to hunger for her, without having seen her? And why, in this tale, was love a curse?

Then I realised that I was concentrating too dutifully on what was present in the text, rather than searching for what was absent. I should, after all, have been looking for the gaps, the silences, for those things that didn't quite make sense, things dense with meaning, well hidden – waiting to be brought to light. Those still, curious moments, where the action subsided and the characters lay exposed, flawed, human even. And that's when I discovered a direction – not in the bulky body of the tale, but on the cusp of it, right there in the introduction. The long and short of what later became my story was all frozen in the first paragraph, like a still from a fascinating film I'd always meant to watch:

Cilydd son of Celyddon Wledig wanted a wife as well born as himself. The woman he wanted was Goleuddydd, daughter of Anlawdd Wledig. After he had slept with her the country went to prayer to see whether they might have an heir. And they had a son through the country's prayers. And from the hour she became pregnant she went mad, and did not go near any dwelling. When her time came, her senses returned to her. This happened in a place where a swineherd was tending a herd of pigs. And out of fear of the pigs the queen gave birth. And the swineherd took the boy until he came to court. And the boy was baptised and was named Culhwch because he was found in a pig run. But the boy was of noble descent, he was cousin to Arthur. And the boy was placed with foster parents.

I realised suddenly that my own tale needn't be Culhwch's quest, or Olwen's for that matter. My instincts drove me to look beyond the tale, behind the tale, to scrutinise those characters that had given rise to the whole sorry situation in the first place. And that's when the more potent questions surfaced, whose answers lay in the writing process itself. Did Culhwch embark on his quest, not so much because of his stepmother's curse, but because of the circumstances of his birth and upbringing? How had losing his mother affected him – having been uprooted in such an unceremonious manner – had it made him crave security, demand to have things resolved? And what of Cilydd, the one left behind, mourning the wife he had once loved so dearly? Did he blame himself somehow, for getting her pregnant in the first place? Why did Goleuddydd become mad in pregnancy? Was it a hormonal imbalance, or something more deep-rooted? How on earth did she end up giving birth in a pigsty?

I put the *Mabinogion* aside for the time being, and began writing, relying only on my memory and impression of the tale. Before I knew it, Cilydd had taken on a life – and a quest – of his own. He

inhabited commonplace territories like super-
markets and high streets and community halls, and
yet somehow still carried the extraordinary landscapes of the Mabinogion deep within him.
Whenever I was unsure where to turn, I would
take a glance once again at the original tale, whose
map seemed to dictate the rest of the scene, whose
signposts directed me to fantastical events which
seemed almost at odds with the ordinariness of my
characters' lives, but which simultaneously made
perfect sense. Occasionally, almost coincidentally,
both tales ended up bumping into each other at
exactly the same place, at a complex fictional cross-
roads. And eventually, as my tale forged its own plot,
the spirit of the telling, and the dark forces driving
the fiction began to resonate with the *Mabinogion's*
storytelling ethos – charging on ahead in bold
realist strides with surreality trailing at its heels,
waiting to bite. How far removed, after all, is a
strange disappearance in a supermarket, or the fall of
the house of the missing, from a world in which
brothers are turned into animals and made to mate,

dead men are brought back alive from the eye of a cauldron and a maiden's virtue is challenged by stepping over a magical rod?

Ultimately I found that Cilydd and Goleuddydd, in many ways, were the original Culhwch and Olwen, and that they were in fact more interesting, damaged and complex than their rather one-dimensional offspring. And although their particular tale presents us with a different quest, one which leaves Culhwch and Ysbaddaden by the wayside and thrusts Cilydd forth as an unlikely hero – both quests are nevertheless bound together, weaving in and out of each other's fictional landscapes, illuminating and shadowing each other, each twist and turn navigating a white trail of hope around the encroaching darkness of the *Mabinogion*.

Fflur Dafydd

Acknowledgements

Thanks are due to my ever-encouraging colleagues at Swansea University, Professor Stevie Davies, Nigel Jenkins, David Britton, and especially Professor Neil Reeve, who made it possible for me to take brief teaching relief in order to become writer-in-residence at Iowa University. Thanks, too, to my agent, Euan Thorneycroft, for his counsel, Owen Sheers for his support, and Peter Florence for being such a vocal advocate of my work. Menna Elfyn and Siân Elfyn Jones, as always, have been my first readers, and I am extremely grateful to them for their speedy reading and feedback. I could also not have asked for a more patient and understanding editor in Penny Thomas, and I am greatly indebted to her for her hard work and precision.

Much of this book was written in the spare bedroom of Sŵn-yr-Einion, Llangain, and my heartfelt gratitude goes to Wendy and Glanmor Evans for allowing me the time and privacy to work, and for feeding and entertaining both myself and my daughter. I am lucky to have such wonderful parents-in-law, just as my daughter is lucky to have such loving grandparents.

GWYNETH LEWIS
THE MEAT TREE

A dangerous tale of desire, DNA, incest and flowers plays out within the wreckage of an ancient spaceship in *The Meat Tree*, an absorbing retelling of one of the best-known Welsh myths by prizewinning writer and poet, Gwyneth Lewis.

An elderly investigator and his female apprentice hope to extract the fate of the ship's crew from its antiquated virtual reality game system, but their empirical approach falters as the story tangles with their own imagination.

By imposing a distance of another 200 years and millions of light years between the reader and the medieval myth, Gwyneth Lewis brings the magical tale of Blodeuwedd, a woman made of flowers, closer than ever before: maybe uncomfortably so.

After all, what man has any idea how sap burns in the veins of a woman?

Gwyneth Lewis was the first National Poet of Wales, 2005-6. She has published seven books of poetry in Welsh and English, the most recent of which is *A Hospital Odyssey*. *Parables and Faxes* won the Aldeburgh Poetry Prize and was also shortlisted for the Forward, as was *Zero Gravity*. Her non-fiction books are *Sunbathing in the Rain: A Cheerful Book on Depression* (shortlisted for the Mind Book of the Year) and *Two in a Boat: A Marital Voyage*.

OWEN SHEERS
WHITE RAVENS

"Hauntingly imaginative..." – Dannie Abse

Two stories, two different times, but the thread of an ancient tale runs through the lives of twenty-first-century farmer's daughter Rhian and the mysterious Branwen... Wounded in Italy, Matthew O'Connell is seeing out WWII in a secret government department spreading rumours and myths to the enemy. But when he's given the bizarre task of escorting a box containing six raven chicks from a remote hill farm in Wales to the Tower of London, he becomes part of a story over which he seems to have no control.

Based on the Mabinogion story 'Branwen, Daughter of Llyr', *White Ravens* is a haunting novella from an award-winning writer.

Owen Sheers is the author of two poetry collections, *The Blue Book* and *Skirrid Hill* (both Seren); a Zimbabwean travel narrative, *The Dust Diaries* (Welsh Book of the Year 2005); and a novel, *Resistance*, shortlisted for the Writers' Guild Best Book Award. *A Poet's Guide to Britain* is the accompanying anthology to Owen's BBC 4 series.

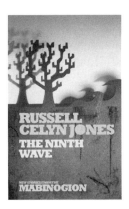

RUSSELL CELYN JONES
THE NINTH WAVE

"A brilliantly-imagined vision of the near future...
one of his finest achievements." – Jonathan Coe

Pwyll, a young Welsh ruler in a post-oil world, finds his inherited
status hard to take. And he's never quite sure how he's drawn into
murdering his future wife's fiancé, losing his only son and
switching beds with the king of the underworld. In this bizarrely
upside-down, medieval world of the near future, life is cheap and
the surf is amazing; but you need a horse to get home again down
the M4.

Based on the Mabinogion story 'Pwyll, Lord of Dyfed', *The Ninth
Wave* is an eerie and compelling mix of past, present and future.
Russell Celyn Jones swops the magical for the psychological, the
courtly for the post-feminist and goes back to Swansea Bay to
complete some unfinished business.

Russell Celyn Jones is the author of six novels. He has won the
David Higham Prize, the Society of Authors Award, and the
Weishanhu Award (China). He is a regular reviewer for several
national newspapers and is Professor of Creative Writing at
Birkbeck College, London.

NIALL GRIFFITHS
THE DREAMS OF MAX & RONNIE

There's war and carnage abroad and Iraq-bound squaddie Ronnie is out with his mates 'forgetting what has yet to happen'. He takes something dodgy and falls asleep for three nights in a filthy hovel where he has the strangest of dreams, watching the tattooed tribes of modern Britain surrounding a grinning man playing war games.

Meanwhile gangsta Max is fed up with life in his favourite Cardiff nightclub, Rome, and chases a vision of the perfect woman in far-flung parts of his country. But as Max loses his heart, his followers fear he may be losing his touch.

Niall Griffiths' retellings of two dream myths from the medieval Welsh Mabinogion cycle reveal an astonishingly contemporary and satirical resonance. Arthurian legend merges with its twenty-first century counterpart in a biting commentary on leadership, conflict and the divisions in British society.

Niall Griffiths was born in Liverpool in 1966, studied English, and now lives and works in Aberystwyth. His novels include *Grits*, *Sheepshagger, Kelly and Victor* and *Stump*, which won Wales Book of the Year, and *Runt*. His non-fiction includes *Real Aberystwyth* and *Real Liverpool*. He also writes reviews, radio plays and travel pieces.

HORATIO CLARE
THE PRINCE'S PEN

The Invaders' drones hear all and see all, and England is now a defeated archipelago, but somewhere in the high ground of the far west, insurrection is brewing.

Ludo and Levello, the bandit kings of Wales, call themselves freedom fighters. Levello has the heart and help of Uzma, from Pakistan – the only other country in the free world. Ludo has a secret, lethal if revealed.

Award-winning author Horatio Clare refracts politics, faith and the contemporary world order through the prism of one of the earliest British myths, the Mabinogion, to ask who are the outsiders, who the infidels and who the enemy within...

Horatio Clare is a writer, radio producer and journalist. Born in London, he grew up on a hill farm in the Black Mountains of South Wales as described in his first book *Running for the Hills*, nominated for the *Guardian* First Book Award and shortlisted for the *Sunday Times* Young Writer of the Year Award. Horatio has written about Ethiopia, Namibia and Morocco, and now divides his time between South Wales, Lancashire and London. His other books include *Sicily through Writers' Eyes*, *Truant: Notes from the Slippery Slope* and *A Single Swallow* for which he was the recipient of a Somerset Maugham Award.